ᛚᛟᚴᛁ

LOKI

Chaos or Catalyst

Lady Wolf

GREEN MAGIC

Green Magic
53 Brooks Road
Street
Somerset
BA16 0PP
England
www.greenmagicpublishing.com

Designed and typeset by Carrigboy, Wells, UK
www.carrigboy.co.uk

ISBN 978 1 915580 08 5

GREEN MAGIC

Introduction

Each day begins with an eruption – a sudden outbreak of something, typically unwelcome or noisy. The beeping of the alarm that says it's time to get out of bed and begin a new day, regardless of how much sleep was obtained, regardless of whether or not one wants to actually leave the safe, comfort and peace of one's bed. Each day begins with an eruption.

After I finished my third book, *Skadi – Mother of Wolves, Goddess of Winter,* my Lover and I went on a pilgrimage to Scotland for two weeks. This was my celebratory, relaxing, enjoyable and fully present holiday. What an amazing two weeks we had exploring once again Edinburgh (my most favorite city) and some of the surrounding towns.

Going on a pilgrimage or holiday is a great way to reset. It was on this trip that my Luv asked me what my next book was. The answer came with only a slight hesitation: "I'm thinking devotional to Loki."

The hesitation came from the fact that Loki was and is associated synonymously with chaos. So, while we wandered around Stirling, I asked myself: was I ready for chaos?

Writing a book is an intense, time-consuming project for any author. For me, it is one best described as invoking through ritual. When I have set intention for a book, the Universe has been pretty complimentary – giving me experiences that are synchronistic and in tune with the topic of each one.

Crafting a devotional book to a figure who is often loathed, resented and blamed for everything meant that there were going to be things that would appear in my life to mirror those attributes and, quite frankly, thrust my life emotionally, spiritually and physically into a state of chaos.

The next day, back in Edinburgh, while stepping off a curb, my Luv hit my shoe just right so that the entire sole popped off – this was the beginning of chaos. My eruption! Was I ready to work through the chaos of writing this book? Not entirely. Was I ready to tromp all over wet Scotland with no sole on my shoe? Not entirely. Either way, this eruption, this decision was going to happen. Now it's up to me to embrace the process or resist …?

> "We adore chaos because
> we love to produce order."
>
> M.C. Escher

This book is dedicated to my friend of thirty years, Amy Michelle Tanner, who put down her warrior sword, let go, let be and flew free away from the cancer that wracked her body in ways unimaginable.

Thank you Amy,
for teaching me to be wild,
for allowing me a space in your life to share in the chaos,
to witness the eruption of fearful tears,
to hold your hand and cradle you on your last day here on this planet.
You gifted me with laughter, friendship and real truths.
Amy, you were and always will be a Giant in my life.
There were many times I witnessed you battle with your body, your mind and your heart.
You taught me to keep going, no matter what: "Don't give up!"
Thank you for being the most chaotic person I've ever met.
Your mayhem touched the lives of so many.
Your passion for life, for family and for your friends is an inspiration.
I will forever cherish those five hours that I was able to hold you, sing to you and share stories with you while your soul began its journey and your body finally found peace from the hell of cancer.
I miss you every day Wild Thang!

Dear Readers

This book is written as my personal devotion to Loki the Trickster.

Call it my year of chaos depicted as a love letter to all that embracing chaos brought to me. Call it a cautionary tale.

Thank you for allowing me to share my journey without judgment and criticism. This book is not factual – I am in no way an expert.

I am no scholar.

For the past thirteen months, I have consciously invoked Loki and at times unwillingly embraced his chaos into my life.

There have been many times that I have regretted this decision. Like my sweet friend, I am no quitter.

Moving through the process of birthing this book has brought about a full shattering in my life on mental, emotional, physical and spiritual levels.

Thank you for taking time to indulge one author in her attempt to shift perspective and offer insights on an individual, a god, a figure who is often misunderstood, scrutinized, villainous and excused from some circles.

My writing process is a ritual or ceremony.

Some of what I say will be repetitive. A wise teacher once told me that "repetition brings conviction." After thirteen months of Loki in my life, I now can see why people looked weary when I mentioned that my next book was dedicated to Loki. After all, who writes a book about the God of Chaos, Mischief and Destruction?

When I first felt the desire to write a book of devotion about Loki, it was with an air of arrogance and intent to piss off those who fear and loathe him. Little did I know at the time that Loki would thrust upon me a madness and force me to fear, loathe or resist these same attributes within myself.

Over the past two decades, I have worked with and embraced many deities and god-like figures. The knowledge gained has been incredible.

Loki shook me the most.

This past year has taught me that there are aspects of Loki that are frightening, but I do not fear him. Loki has become a friend.

Chaos a Lover.

All Hail Loki!!!!!

Contents

CHAPTER ONE

Myths as Metaphors

We begin with a story. A telling of good versus evil. There are beasties, baddies, heroes and saints. It seems that every myth has familiar characters and similar narratives. We as humans cling to these stories as truths. But what really is a myth? Are they metaphors that offer us insight – or manipulations meant to control? Can we accept them as both?

The dictionary defines myth as: *A traditional story, especially one concerning the early history of a people or explaining some natural or social phenomenon, and typically involving supernatural beings or events.* Human beings are fascinated if not somewhat obsessed with creation myths. We want to know our origin. We need to know!

Can we ever really know? The answer is sadly, no. Unless time travel becomes a reality, there is no way of actually knowing how humans came to be. We can look at the scientific possibilities or the religious stories but there is no concrete proof. It comes down to the individual and what will fill your soul.

As a constant student of life, the whole creation myth or 'what came first, the chicken or the egg?" really hasn't been much of a concern for me. My focus is on the day-to-day. Growing up, I was taught (like most) in school about the evolution of man; and in church I was taught something very contradictory.

Ultimately, I had to shrug my shoulders and be okay with the fact that I was never going to know, so why waste time and energy when I could be spending that energy and time on living my life to its fullest? In my efforts, to live fully became a vital part of my equation.

Growing up, myths were a part of our school curriculum – mostly the Greek myths, which never really interested me. I know there were hidden metaphors and lessons to be found woven into the tapestries of each story but the Greek myths never excited me. In high school, I felt a pull to the Celtic myths and legends and then the Norse sagas came into my spectrum and I felt a spark.

As a high priestess and coven mother in the past decade, I have had many "new to the craft" students come to me and ask me where to begin. Let's face it, there is so much available and it can become overwhelming if one tries to embrace all the many pantheons. My answer to those seeking was to discover the individual's history or their story. Learn about where they came from and start with those myths and legends from their bloodline.

This has been a helpful tool for me. So naturally, as a teacher, I like to share what I have learned and need to learn and practice the most. My DNA analysis results revealed Northwestern Europe, Ireland, Wales, Norway and Scotland. For me, it just made sense that I would feel a connection with Celtic, Scottish and Norse pantheons, myths, legends and sagas.

My DNA results would essentially open up a doorway for me to begin my exploration of where my roots began. Lucky for me, my father spent extended time doing research and genealogy for the Church, so he had access to tools that surpassed my google search button. There were afternoons where I drove the 45 minutes to meet up with my dad and, together, we would journey into our ancestors to see who made the journey from Ireland to the States and whose lineage we could be traced back to. This was an amazing experience and life-changing in many ways.

When my students would begin tracing their roots and spending time with pantheons that were in their bloodline, they too felt a strong sense of belonging. In essence, they were researching their own creation myths.

While there is no right or wrong way to begin, as we are all individuals doing the best we can, this technique has been very helpful for me. The important thing to ask oneself is: what will give you greater hope, insight and understanding? Knowing the origin of mankind or knowing your own individual origin?

Edith Hamilton, author of *Mythology*, refers to the Greek myths as a general way of showing how the human race thought and felt at the time: "Through it, according to this view, we can retrace the path from civilized man who lives so far from nature, to man who lived in close companionship with nature; and the real interest of myths is that they lead us back to a time when the world was young and people had a connection with the earth, with trees and seas and flowers and hills, unlike anything we ourselves can feel."

There is a natural attraction amongst the myths and those who are disconnecting from Christian dogma to Pagan. I would agree with Edith when she talks about how myths lead us back to that earth connection. The myths give us a new way of looking at the earth, trees, waters and animals as a very part of our physical selves. They help connect the dots of earth, air, fire, water and spirit.

MYTHS HAVE BEEN CATEGORIZED INTO FOUR BASIC THEORIES:

Rational, functional, structural and psychological.

Rational myth theory states that myths were made to better understand natural events and forces that occurred in the everyday lives of people, with the gods & goddesses controlling all of these natural happenings.

Functional myth theory talks about how myths were used to teach morality and social behavior. What to do and what not to do. In teaching morality, the consequences of the behavior acted out within the myth is applied as the real lesson.

Structural myth theory discusses the emotions involved. They spotlight the good and the bad.

This theory of structure creates a divide amongst the mind/soul and the human relationship with aspects of nature. Structural myth is focused on the duality of human nature. In the myths, we see characters who experience conflict – action and outcome both felt physically and emotionally. Structuralism also brings into light how the individual character activates a mind/soul attribute and connection to objects such as trees, flowers, rocks and water.

Psychological myth theory acknowledges that myths are based on human emotion and that they come from the human subconscious mind. When we look at the myths in a manner of observation then we can see how characters expressed themselves and we can relate and give explanations as to why we feel the way we are feeling or why we are acting in such a way.

Myths help us to connect universally. Myths are stories that through verbal and written retellings can teach us about different cultures, their day-to-day, beliefs and ways of survival. They are metaphors that each culture shares, as each culture has their own unique yet very similar stories.

Metaphor is defined as: *a figure of speech that describes an object or action in a way that isn't literally true, but helps explain an idea or make a comparison.* When we look at all the different creation myths, they are not literally true – again, who really knows the truth? These myths are stories that help to explain the possibility of mankind's beginning and origin. As these myths progress, they are filled with lessons that can be applied through comparisons to our own lives. My favorite quote about legends and myths comes from the Disney movie, *Brave*: "Legends are lessons, they ring with truth."

Metaphors suggest comparisons, although they don't explicitly state a comparison. Myths are metaphors. Metaphors can often reveal truths that are deeper and more lasting, but harder to unpack. We cannot take the metaphor (or the myth) literally and expect to understand its full symbolic value.

Scholars can argue and debate, individuals can argue and debate and modern-day Pagans can and do argue and debate about the importance of myths. As individuals, each of us will formulate an equally unique connection with the myths and our unique connection should not be open for debate.

We look to myths because they create a possible answer to our human questions through comparative experiences and characters. Why Loki? What comparisons can be found within the sagas? For me, the question isn't "why Loki?" – it's really "why not Loki?"

In the Archaic period, **Chaos** was the first thing to exist. From Chaos, life began. Loki and Chaos just appeared in the myths, out of a sudden eruption. Chaos was born. Edith Hamilton describes Loki as: "not a god, but the son of a Giant and wherever he came, trouble followed. Norse mythology and Greek mythology together give a clear picture of what people were like, from whom comes a major part of our spiritual and intellectual inheritance."

Writing a book of devotion to Loki makes sense. Humans long for understanding and connection to the old myths of our youth and our ancestry. Chaos is the instigator, the catalyst of our beginning. Chaos is what triggers reactions, actions and these result in consequences.

WE MUST HAVE CHAOS!

Myths by definition are fictional – they are stories. Stories are told by storytellers and, over time and through oral traditions, each teller naturally adds a bit of their own personal interpretation to the story. We the listeners are responsible for how we interpret each story, which means that we are responsible if we anchor into them as truth or fiction. Myths are not factual.

When we look at myths in this manner, we can see that it is human nature to create an adversary, a baddie, someone to blame. Loki is that persona in the Norse myths, just like the devil is that same persona (the beastie, the literal fallen angel) in Christianity. It is important to understand and be okay with knowing that creation myths and characters in religions are also fictional – fictional until proven factual. This will upset some readers.

Humans create adversaries, just like we create stories. We need a hero or "savior" – someone to look up to – and also someone to steer clear of. Myths as metaphors become mirrors that show us, the individuals, that we personally possess hero and villain attributes. Maybe our perception and holding on to these stories as fact creates a blockage in our personal ability to embrace our own inner and outer hero and villain?

The Norse myths highlight Loki as a baddie, the devil, mischievous and someone to loathe, to dare not speak his name and to avoid. But isn't it up to us as the readers and listeners of the myths to formulate opinions for ourselves? I think so. Anytime I am told to simply blindly believe something, my inner hunches raise and I ask myself: "why should I just believe that?"

If myths are written and shared to inspire, teach and anchor us into a way of living and thinking that gives us reason and purpose here on Earth then we should be looking at each character in myth through the same eyes that we want strangers and friends to see us with.

Loki is a friend to me. For some, he is only seen through the eyes of the storytellers – he is a villain. The intention of this book is to shed light on duality and to hopefully encourage readers to formulate their own perspectives, ideals and practices, rather than hold onto someone else's words (even mine, the Author's) as factual and the only way.

Loki is a friend to me of the truest kind. When I allow the synchronicities to surface through my own writing process then I can see clearly that my cherished friend Amy, who this book is dedicated to, was my Loki in the flesh. She was the kind of friend who had a bad reputation, a false story told by tellers who didn't know her. As a true friend, she would challenge, poke, prod, nudge and annoy with love. She would instigate and encourage all her friends to live their lives to the fullest. She was the bad guy to many and a savior to thousands. Loki is the same.

We create adversaries because we need someone to blame – we need a fall guy. There is not a myth written that does not contain an adversary. Why? If myths are metaphors, then who really is the bad guy? I believe that we are the bad guys in our own stories. We have within us a darkness, a shadow or unpopular side that is hated and loathed not just by others but by ourselves.

Weeks ago, I made a post on my social media asking about myths and their personal value. It was astonishing to me how little of a response I received. I could only speculate that individuals were embarrassed by their personal attachment to myths and felt unsafe in responding. The people that did choose to respond spoke of their willingness to believe that myths were fiction but they had allowed certain myths to become truths. There is nothing wrong with that. It's in our human nature.

Most of us were taught myths as metaphors and life lessons from our childhood. Look at the stories of *Hansel and Gretel*, *Goldilocks and the Three Bears*, and *The Boy Who Cried Wolf*. These were stories/myths with actual lessons taught alongside them. Myths from different pantheons and cultures share similarities.

The lessons might not be spelled out or presented to us in a classroom setting but the lessons are there for us the individuals to apply or not.

One individual who responded to my post said that they looked to myths as opportunities to ask questions...to seek more insight. Another individual expressed that they enjoyed myths, especially ones pertaining to their actual ancestry, as a way of creating connection between the beliefs of ancestors, the land and past – a way of "guessing" how this individual's ancestors lived and possibly what they believed or practiced. To this individual, myths were a window into the past.

The third person to respond stated that myths (especially in religion) were harmful and, through the retelling from Church leaders, became toxic and harmful and created characters who were unobtainable, unkind and problematic, yet were to be worshiped and followed as truth and the only way.

If we are here to live a life journey experience that is unique to us then we need to hold ourselves accountable for believing the storytellers who captivated and ensnared us, or manipulated us. We chose to believe them. The myths are stories, it's that simple. We are the ones responsible for interpreting them as anything more than just that.

Throughout this book, you will read stories about Loki. Most will highlight him in a negative way. It is my intent to poke and prod you the reader to see that you can shift the perspective. So "leaders" in modern-day Pagan/Heathen groups say Loki is to be avoided, he to be blamed, he is to not even be mentioned. These are simply people stating their opinion. This book is one author's opinion and cautionary tale of the past thirteen months that I have spent researching and embracing Loki as Chaos. It is my hope that you, the reader, will take time to formulate your own opinion. At the end of this book, some of you may continue to dislike Loki but some of you just may begin to embrace him as a friend. Again, this is my interpretation and not factual.

> "The power of myths doesn't come from the stories or the storyteller. The power comes from the reader's interpretation and implementation of the metaphoric mirror within the myth."

CHAPTER TWO

Birth of Destruction

LOKI – IS HE GOD, DEVIL, OUTCAST, BROTHER, CHAOS OR CATALYST?

In order to really get to know anyone, it is important to become acquainted with the landscape they grew up in. When it comes to Loki, it is best to honor that he is the landscape of his birthing – just as our landscape and upbringing play pivotal parts in how we respond and engage with the world around us.

Loki is the son of one of the Jotunns (or Giants), Farbauti; his mother being the Goddess Laufey. We know the Land of Giants to be one of the nine worlds featuring deep hidden forests, untamed wilderness and grim, uninviting high mountaintops; a realm of the unknown. The Giant peoples (or Jotunns) are described as hideous, fierce and ugly monsters who survive off the flesh of men. While some dispute that Laufey the mother was a goddess, she has been widely accepted as one of the Jotunns.

Farbauti has been mentioned as the "Cruel Striker" and Laufey, one of the Asynjar or Aesir, has "needle" attached to her name. We see two distinct characteristics in his parents; one being destructor through force and one being able to craft or create.

So Loki is born of possibly two Giants and classified as hideous and frightful. Not quite the Tom Hiddleston that Marvel offers us. *The Prose Edda* offers us a different take on his appearance – that being "tall, lanky of figure with either strawberry blonde or fiery red hair," and at other times he is mentioned as being "of scarred face, cracked lips" – the consensus being that Loki was not ugly but rather beautiful. Loki seems to just randomly appear, rather than having any kind of origin story.

Imagine, if you will, a large snow-covered mountain spewing molten, hot lava. Picture that lava flowing down the side of the mountain with such force, yet grace. This literal fire from the mountain erupts with such force as to demand the attention of all who are nearby. As this liquid flame slithers, it destroys everything it touches. A force! At the base of the mountain, the water from the sea crashes, thick layers of ice sheets. Another force! Together, fire and ice collide into one incredible display of the polar opposite elements creating a cataclysmic event happening in the center – "The Birth of Loki."

For me, this is how I see Loki coming into existence. Could his Giant father, Farbauti, be the mountain? His Giant mother the sea? Let's keep in mind that no one knows. All we have is speculation. The somewhat cherished *Prose Edda*, written by Snorri Sturluson (an early thirteenth century Christian historian) some 200 years after the supposed happenings of the ancient Norse gods, are not factual but they are insightful.

Loki for me represents the chaos of two *violent natural elemental events*; the definition of cataclysm. He is a force of Nature. He is that second between the hot and the cold. The shudder and the shock! Think of sitting in a hot tub feeling your muscles relax, sweat trickling down your brow and then you suddenly jump into an ice bath. That jolting eruption to your physical and emotional senses in a fully cataclysmic assault is Loki.

His name has many different meanings, such as "knot, tangle, trickster, lock, light-bringer, fire." While some will argue that he is not a *fire god*, as that title pertains more to "Logi" – again, I will ask: who really knows and does it really matter? Loki has an arsenal of diverse titles, such as "God of Chaos, Shapeshifter, God of Mischief, Cunning One, Brother of Odin, Husband, Father, Mother, Murderer, He who Schemes, Light-Bringer, Father of Monsters, God of Temptation, God of Sex, Evil One, Originator of Deceits, Disgrace of All Gods and Men." There are a mix of contradictions with his titles and names.

Loki is a multifaceted and complicated individual. Is this a bad thing? While diving into my own inner chaos, I narrow things down to perspective as an individual. My personal definition of chaos will be drastically different from another's definition. It is my belief that we are all multifaceted and oftentimes very complicated. Whether that is good or bad is open to interpretation.

Most have heard the phrase, "what is normal to the spider is chaos to the fly." This phrase highlights that ultimately, when forming any kind of conclusion based on a personal experience, it is up to the individual to decipher the intention of the spider or the fly.

Loki, like the spider, is cunning, charming and manipulative. Or is he? The fly is supposedly a representation of innocence, or could the fly be arrogantly unaware? Is Loki the spider or is he the fly? Loki is so fascinating in his inability to fit into any kind of mold that I think there are many that are repulsed by him and many that are intrigued by him. He to me is both – spider and fly.

In Diana Paxson's book, *Essential Asatru*, she has this to say about Loki: "Steer clear of Loki if you have a problem with ambiguity. However you relate to reality, you should deal with him carefully. Bear in mind that Loki is a trickster, and unless you are experienced in dealing with chaotic forces, it might be better to not attract his attention."

Ambiguity is the quality of being open to more than one interpretation.

I myself am passionately inspired by his dualities and complicated unknowns. For me, Loki is a breath of fresh air despite the chaos. When I started my journey into working with Loki, it began from a need to destroy structure and routine. Oftentimes, when we are told to steer clear from something, that warning is the instigating factor to rebel and do the opposite.

There are numerous deities of old that are invited, despite similar warnings, such as The Morrigan, Hecate, Kali and Sekhmet to list a few. The warning is really asking those who are doing the seeking to remember that there are consequences. If you invite a shattering and expect things to not break, that is completely on you. There is no one outside of self to blame.

In seeking some kind of scrambled escape from normalcy, looking to Loki was "Entering the Birth of Destruction." In order to really move forward towards a completely new direction, one must "create or cause so much damage to something that it no longer exists or can be repaired." Think of the Tower card side by side with the Death card from the tarot deck, instigated or triggered by the Fool card. In order to birth, one must die, or allow things in their life to die.

The Tower card depicts a tall brick tower being struck by lightning, flames falling down along with two figures screaming as they are about to hit the ground below. At the top of the tower is a crown being toppled by fire. Destruction! Chaos! The key is the foundation which has held the tower up for so long and still stands.

The Death card depicts an armed skeleton, the harbinger of death riding on a horse, holding a black and white banner. This card signifies that one phase is ending and a new one being birthed.

As a midwife who has attended numerous births, I know there is a line a woman walks when she is letting her old life and body die in order to bring about a new life. Destruction can be both frightening and beautiful. Birth can be frightening and beautiful – just like death. While it is scary to imagine a life without that person in it, the beauty is there when they can finally be rid of the suffering and be at peace. There is balance in these life transitions that we don't really see in the moment as we are engrossed in the chaos – those chaos-heightened emotions.

Loki to me is very much these three cards. Later, you will see him introduced as another tarot card. For me, he is the tower, he is the death-bringer and he is the fool. This is not a reference to the physical death of one's mortal experience; rather it is the emotional and spiritual death of expectations, inhibitions, insecurities and beliefs that may no longer serve one on an individual basis. Oftentimes in our short life, we need to be given permission, prompting and encouragement to let these things die in order to activate changes, whether they be subtle or massive.

In calling upon Loki, there were certain beliefs that I had to sit with and re-evaluate. In reality, this act of reevaluation is a daily process. What worked for us as individuals yesterday, or even today, might not work for us tomorrow. It was really no surprise that my next book, following my *Skadi* book, would be devoted to Loki. After all, it was during my studies of Skadi that I first encountered Loki.

Activating the passion of the fire element and the ability to pause and not react with the element of ice, I entered energetically and spiritually the realm of Loki. The Chaos. I had chosen to give birth to my own destruction of old belief patterns and routines. This I would continue for the next thirteen months.

Walking a pathway of choices on both sides of me; one representing what I had gained so far and the other representing the unforeseen possibilities that would require time, energy and accountability – both triggered some fear and some excitement. Again, dualities at play. Night and day, dark and light, good and bad; it all comes down to perspective and the willingness to keep moving forward.

Would my decision to invoke Loki into my life piss people off? Yes! In the end does it matter? Other people's opinions of me are really none of my business. Nor do I care to hear them. When I erupt into each new day, I do so for me.

Loki is synonymous with pandemonium, turmoil, chasm, bedlam, anarchy, uproar, muddle, scramble, jumble, clutter, disarray, shambles, topsy-turvy, snafu, chaos! Can any of these be actually avoided? No! Life is chaotic. Life is destructive. Life is dualities. Life is hot and cold.

The best advice for beginning this journey with Loki is to *expect the unexpected*. When one expects chaos then one is not as easily provoked or offended when chaos happens. Learning to go with the flow of things rather than fight or flight is the essence of inviting Loki into your life. It is the key concept. Invite chaos, expect chaos and go with the flow.

Just prior to my winter Scotland holiday, I invited a few people over for a ceremonial gathering dedicated to Loki. The intent was to help clear away the old and create a space for new beginnings.

We circled up outdoors in what is commonly referred to as the Faery Circle located on the Desert Healing Sanctuary healing center that I live on and facilitate. We began with stating the intention of the event. The Loki candle with the Chaos symbol was lit and a meditation journey followed.

The instant Loki's name was mentioned, the wind began to blow with such incredible force. This was not a slight subtle breeze, this was the kind of wind that seemed to blow from every direction. The wind was so loud rustling through the trees that while leading the meditation it felt like I had to yell. This torrentuous wind continued throughout the entire meditation and stopped immediately once the meditation was complete. This was no coincidence.

Embracing the wind was his way (and my way) of blowing out old belief patterns that, while they benefited me at the time, were no longer going to help me move forward on my journey into chaos and birthing destruction in my own close-minded state of comfort. Wind magick is excellent to harness anytime an individual wants to blow out and away the things holding them down. For me, as an individual, I was currently at a crossroads and in preparation for holiday and I really wanted to set the intention of letting go in order to create space to receive. The wind helped tremendously.

INVITING LOKI MEDITATION

❖✲❖

Create a container for your meditation.
A time and place where you will be undisturbed.
Sit with intention to invite Loki and bring your
awareness to your breath.

❖✲❖

Begin with a slow, conscious inhale to the count of four and exhale to the count of four.

(Repeat this breath pattern for at least four breath cycles)

Allow your physical body to create its own rhythm and wave pattern as you consciously focus on your inhales and exhales. By focusing on your breath, you give yourself time and permission to enter a state of the present moment. In this state of focused breathing, you are beginning to physically relax and mentally prepare yourself to journey into the realm of possibilities.

In your mind's eye, your intuitive realm, picture yourself standing on a pathway. On each side of the pathway are tall trees and thick forest foliage. Before you, in the distance, are two large mountains, very distinct. One is covered in ice and snow, the other is a volcano with red, molten lava cascading down it. Each mountain represents an element, a realm of chaos, unpredictable occurrences and contradictions.

You find that you are walking on the path that leads right between both mountains. You are literally going to venture between fire and ice. This "in-between" represents chaos – the unknown or the ever-knowing.

As you make your way upon the path, the mountains are getting closer and larger. You can smell the lava. You can feel the chill of the ice mountain and the heat from the volcano.

Yet, like a magnet you are pulled forward, a tug to connect with both mountains.

Fire and ice are both catalysts for change. They move, flow, chill, shape, break, destroy, build, freeze and burn – just like life. You can't escape, so you keep walking. Each step gifting you with the mirror of understanding. The realms of fire and ice are no different than erupting into each new day. For each new day is filled with the unknown and the unpredictable.

Once you reach the center of the pathway directly between the fire and ice mountains, you sit down and begin to light your own fire. As you add sticks to the flames, you feel the presence of another. A cloaked figure has come to join you at your fire. The figure says nothing, only watches the flames as they dance. So, you sit and say nothing. Together you watch the flames as they dance. The fire represents you. Your flame is as tall as you want it to be. Your chill or heat is all up to you.

(Pause)

The hooded figure beside you begins to move and the body begins to quiver and shake. The cloak falls down to the ground and you find yourself staring at a coyote. The coyote circles the fire, circling you and runs off down the path that leads far beyond, between the fire and ice mountains. Gone out of sight.

Loki the shifter, the catalyst, the birth-giver of destruction, the instigator. Loki is of mischief, mayhem and pandemonium. Loki is who was seated at your fire. But why? The answer is really in the question of "why not?"

Life is chaotic. Beautifully unpredictable. In life, we have choices to react with heat, passion and fire – or we can freeze and chill out. Choices. Our ability to respond, reach or not react. Our power to engage, disengage or move beyond. Loki is a teacher, mentor; he is candid and erratic – just like life lessons.

Bring your awareness back to your breath. Breathing in gratitude for the mirror of the coyote. Exhaling out and away the desire to control the journey.

Both Loki and coyote offer us perspective and mirrors of flexibility, determination and they encourage us to see the humor in the turmoil. It is my intent with this devotional book that you, the reader, can formulate your own connection with Loki. A connection outside of what you are told is right and what you are told is wrong. After all, one's connection with any of the gods/deities is not open for discussion, nor is it necessary to explain.

Formulating a connection with a practice, religion or god (or in Loki's case, maybe not a god) is for the individual. There is no right or wrong, there is only doing that which works for you on a personal level. I've been badgered into debates and attempted arguments on "my way versus your way or the way according to so-and-so or this book or that book or she said or he said." Gatekeepers and self-proclaimed experts are everywhere, especially today with the rise of modern Paganism.

My response is always the same: "my beliefs and practices are not open for judgment as they fulfill me and that's all that matters." When each new day erupts, I am the one that chooses to embrace that eruption or resist it. The day will go on regardless.

We the individuals living our lives are the ones who determine the outcome of each day, opportunity and moment. Loki has shown us a way to really be catalysts for our own change and to expect the unexpected. Again, he is both spider and fly – as are we.

Realize that you have the capability to become consciously aware, that you are the only one who can instigate change within your life – so start now. In her book, *Essential Asatru*, Diana Paxson sums it up best with this: "Just as friendship comes in different degrees, so does the intensity of devotion to one's god." Your devotion is yours to establish, to invest in and to be accountable for.

CHAPTER THREE

Chaos!

Loki and chaos seem to go hand in hand. They blend into one and the same. What is chaos? In the dictionary, chaos is defined as: *complete disorder and confusion*. When you hear the word chaos, what comes to mind? For me, chaos is a physical disorder. Have you ever been caught in a windstorm with gusts so strong you find it hard to catch your breath? Here in the desert, those windstorms happen all too often. On an emotional and physical level, one's individual definition of and experience with chaos will always be different.

Shortly after those two weeks in Scotland, I arrived home with what I thought was vertigo. After a few days, the feeling of physically being imbalanced didn't go away. A series of processes of elimination followed. I went to an ear, nose and throat doctor, an eye doctor and herbalist. Nothing helped. What I physically was feeling wasn't a spinning sensation but rather a rocking sensation that I soon began to describe as a *boat* day. My body felt like it was rocking on a boat all the time. Even when lying down, it felt like the bed was swaying.

Not being a boat person, this sensation of constant swaying soon began to take its toll on me emotionally. Being a naturally active person, I found it challenging to do my daily yoga while feeling like I was swaying. Time went by, months filled with pockets of depression, moments with no symptoms, and days that quite literally scared me. I was in a state of chaos within my mind and body.

Mal de Debarquement is a rare and often mistreated vestibular disorder. It shows up suddenly and often leaves suddenly. I've only been living with this now for several months, thirteen months to be exact. What I have learned is that chaos can be one of our most informative teachers – just like Loki.

This syndrome, as I call it (rather than dis-ease), is mine, it's in my body, only I can feel it and it's now categorized by the medical profession as a "disorder". For me, each day is a boat day, on some days the waves are more intense and on others they are calmer.

Shifting my perspective, changing my eating habits and doing more balancing exercises and physical therapy has allowed me to thrive whilst in this state of inner and physical chaos. We as humans are actively participating in chaos management on a daily basis. As creatures well capable of adapting, we can do hard things. Accepting the fact that there was no medication that would automatically bring balance back into my physical and mental state forced me to create my own kind of medicine. Had I resisted this new dis-ease and anchored into fear, my results would be much different.

While browsing websites devoted to chaos, I came across a blog that offered some good tips on "how to manage chaos without going insane." The first five tips are super-easy and within our grasp as individuals:

1. Not all chaos is created equal.
2. You can't control everything, but you can control your environment.
3. Create good habits.
4. No success is too small to celebrate.
5. Give yourself a break.

You may wonder what chaos management has to do with Loki? Well, the answer is: everything! Loki is chaos, but is he really? Loki is well-known in the myths and sagas for stirring up and creating chaos. So, he as an individual may not really be chaos but he may be the instigator of chaos or he may be the essence or attribute of chaos. Why?

It has come to my attention that in the 43 years of living in this current existence, the moments of chaos and disorder that I have personally experienced have been my greatest teachers. Think back to your school days, those teachers that you loathed were often the ones that made the most impact, even if it was resisted. These teachers made a lasting impression.

These cataclysmic moments of upheaval, where we often feel tested to our limits, typically occur when we are battling something alone. This kind of intensity takes us to those deep, dark and frightening caves within our psyche where we feel defeated and hopeless. In the past thirteen months, I have learned to love this imbalanced disorder. Not because of how it makes me feel as, let's face it, who wants to feel like they are swaying on a boat 24/7 but I have learned to love it because of my capability to endure with compassion the hard boat days and to really make the most of the mild days. Living present in the moment is where the magic happens.

Looking at the power of wind; if you have ever been in the middle of a windstorm then you know that it can feel like it's sucking the very air needed to breathe. The panic sets in and we naturally want to run indoors to escape the wind. What if we just closed our eyes and allowed the wind to offer us an energetic shower, a cleansing, and we trusted that our body would adapt because we *will do* so? Surrender is the way to really thrive in chaos.

In the Disney show, *Loki,* there is a scene that describes Loki as being "burdened with glorious purpose." That purpose is to challenge the status quo, to create havoc, to test, to challenge and to scheme against the normalcy of society. Loki is the baddie we are taught to hate and be repulsed by. Yet, he carries this weight of unfair judgment and his chaos is what holds all things in balance.

His glorious purpose in mythology seems to be inviting not just the fellow gods but mere mortals to either embrace the disorder, the chaos or to resist. We know that the things we resist in life will persist until we have overcome them. It is beautiful knowing that when we surrender, the greatest shifts occur and are able to occur. Sometimes we need to simply see that chaos is merely the beginning of change. We need chaos to shake us out of the complacency and comfort of the mundane in order for us to expand and thrive.

CHAOS MAGICK is a contemporary magical Neo-Pagan practice developed in England in the 1970s. This practice is a blend of traditional occult and applied postmodernism, implementing skepticism and belief as a tool. This kind of tradition rejects the existence of truth, using a more agnostic approach (agnostic meaning a person who believes that nothing is known or can be known of the existence or nature of God or a god). There are a few rules in chaos magick that are quite fascinating:

1. There are no rules.
2. Nothing is true. Everything is permitted.
3. Belief is a tool for achieving effects.
4. The 4th rule is the 1st rule with emphasis on the 2nd and 3rd rules.

LOKI in myth and legend is notorious for causing mischief. Was he bored? Or was he a mastermind? Throughout this book, you will see that my personal view of Loki is that he is a catalyst by definition – *a person or thing that precipitates an event.*

Loki simply pushed, nudged and helped get things done! Yes, more often than not it was at the expense of others but still the task at hand was completed. His motive was often self-preservation. How many times in your life have you sacrificed someone else or something else for your own good? For your own survival? If you think never then you may want to sit with that denial and arrogance for a bit.

We are all living in a state of self-preservation. We are living our individual lives for ourselves, not for anyone else. As individuals, we can choose to thrive, barely survive, succeed, fail or give up our energy for the sake of others who are simply living for themselves. It all comes down to daily choices.

> "Chaos and uncertainty ensure no plan goes
> according to play."

Think of moments in your life that have been unbelievably chaotic. You obviously survived those as you were able to later look back at them. What did you do in those moments? More often than not, when faced with the uncertainty and chaos of life, we choose to either engage or surrender when, ultimately, we are not doing simply one or the other but a beautiful blending of the two.

As a god (again, debated), Loki was neither completely good nor fully evil. He was neither complete chaos nor complete calm. He wasn't just hot or cold. He was neither balanced nor completely unstable. His main objective was to stir things up a bit and create some havoc.

Chaos is the realm of the dark gods, the unpredictable and unknown. Chaos has been described as a timeless, formless, endless plane of nightmares. Chaos is both an adjective and a noun. We know in Greek mythology that Chaos is the primordial being that sets all things into motion.

We humans give far too much credit to figures in mythology. We give far too much energy to "god-like" beings that we as humans have given that title to in the first place. Were there ever gods? Was Loki actually a being that walked amongst us in human physical form? Or, like all the other deities from old myths, legends and oral traditions, were these figures just characters in stories to metaphorically inspire us?

What is it about Loki and his chaos that inspires you or repulses you, and why? The power comes from how you internalize those attributes and relate to them on a personal level.

Catherine Beyer wrote a pretty interesting article concerning chaos magic, she states that: "Chaos magic is difficult to define because definitions are composed of common components. By definition, chaos magic has no common components. Chaos magic is about using whatever ideas and practices are helpful to you at the moment, even if they contradict the ideas and practices you used previously."

I personally love this because it means that, as a practitioner of magic, it is the individual that creates their own blend of practices. As an individual who was ordained in the Wiccan traditions Dianic, Eclectic and Alexandrian, there were defined ways to "accurately" set one's altar, specific deities to call upon and how to cast one's circle. While for some these "how-to" instructions can be very helpful, for others like myself they began to feel very constricting.

Anchoring into just *one way* of practice or religion is very damaging. We have seen this with the rise of Christianity. If one does not conform to that *one way* of practice or religion, there is persecution, judgment and ridicule. Take a look back at accurate history and you will see just what happened to anyone who didn't want to embrace Jesus as the one and only God or son of God.

Chaos magick gives us perspective and opportunities without the boxes and stipulations of the "proper" or "correct" *how-to's*. It is liberating! Loki is a liberator. He encourages new perspectives and what we see from the myths and sagas is quite a bit of resistance and projection of blame when things do not go as planned.

There is a complexity in ceremonial magic/the traditional system of intellectual magic defined as: "ritual magic, a highly disciplined form of magic in which ceremony and ritual become the central tools used in the magical operation. In the pre-twentieth century form, ceremonial magic's rites were religious actions."

These rites, while unlimited, were bound by the proper "how-to's." As a ceremonial priestess (which is just a fancy way of saying that I am an ordained high priestess and I lead ceremonies), I was trained by mentors and high priestesses on particular ways to cast circles, set up altars and which deities were best to call upon. Instruction was part of my training. While good, it can also be limiting.

In chaos magic, none of those "how-to's" matter. Catherine Beyer coined it up in one paragraph: "Tapping into magic is personal, willful and psychological. Ritual puts the worker in the right frame of mind, but has no value outside of that. Words have no inherent power to them."

Words, just like ancient gods, have power because we as humans give them that. Rituals possess an energetic shift because we believe that they will, so we help raise collective energy to support that ideal of feeling the shift.

As one who has been leading ceremonial magical rites for the past decade, I can honestly say that I prefer group magic because of the intense energy that is invited when others are joining together with a similar unscripted intent. My struggle is the expectation of structure and the "correct" *how-to's*. The past decade has gifted me with incredible learning opportunities and many amazing teachers. Loki/Coyote and Chaos have taught me the most.

Laughter in moments of upheaval is most rewarding. When planning a ritual time and service is offered and it can be exhausting. Loki/Coyote/Chaos has taught me that the best rituals are not planned, there is no outline. Just a "go with it" and feel approach. Be present in the unknown.

When one opens up space or creates a container for group participation there is an uneasy sense of anticipation. Questions go through the mind of everyone. Questions like "What do I say? What am I supposed to do? What if I fuck it all up and ruin the ritual for everyone?" These pockets of internal self doubt actually unite the group because every single person has had their *first* group ritual experience or is about to and there is commonality and comfort with sharing these doubts.

Asking strangers or well-seasoned practitioners to each share the unscripted ritual is like brewing a magnificent stew where each individual represents their own unique ingredient. At the end of the ritual this stew is more delicious because each individual added a bit of themselves. Group ritual is my most favorite because it is unpredictable and at times a bit untamed.

We tend to forget that life is ritual. Everything we do throughout each day is our own unique ritual. From the way we stir our coffee, shower, drive to how we interact with others. Group ritual is catered to a specific intention oftentimes discussed in advance and anchored into the current season. Collectively we bring our unique, authentic rituals and combine them in a group setting.

CHAOS GROUP RITUAL:

Invite your likeminded friends or even strangers to attend a group ritual celebrating a particular season. Encourage guests to bring an item that they feel compliments the season and dress in a way that shows off the energy of the season. Circle up, take some deep breaths to allow everyone to settle into the current experience and disconnect from anything mundane that will create a distraction.

Invite guests to popcorn out words or phrases that sum up how they feel about the particular season. Then allow the energy to flow. Be open and welcome the unpredictable chaos by inviting guests in no particular order to enter the center of the circle and physically, emotionally embody the particular season, placing their chosen item on a group altar.

You will have some guests that are more vocal, and some will be more physical in their embodiment of the season. The ritual may feel scattered with moments of low energy as ego surfaces in the state of self-doubt. The key with chaos magick is to allow and encourage each guest to be themselves, NOT to act how they think they should. There is no right or wrong way of doing rituals in a chaos setting. The ritual becomes chaos by allowing individuals a platform to be their fully unhinged selves.

CHAPTER FOUR

Catalyst

Catalyst is, by the Oxford's dictionary definition: "a person or thing that precipitates an event." In this chapter, let's dive into ALL the many things that Loki did to precipitate or help bring about an event. There are many who believe, like myself, that Loki is the ultimate catalyst.

"Loki is the originator, the instigator, and the finisher of stories: i.e. the catalyst."

When we take time to dive into the myths and sagas, we have one very common figure throughout – Loki. One would think that someone who is at the center of all the major Norse myths would be appreciated but in actuality devotion, or rather repulsion, is pretty divided by practitioners of Norse Paganism.

My devotion is anchored into gratitude and admiration. Years ago, an interested Norse Pagan from Northern Utah reached out to me to inquire about the events we hosted at the Utah Goddess Temple (now called the Desert Healing Sanctuary). Being a former Law Officer, in this world of shady characters, I did a bit of sleuthing on this person's social media page before responding. This person was wearing a Mjolnir "Thor's Hammer" around their neck in their profile picture. A very common artifact of jewelry amongst modern-day Heathens and Nordic practitioners, myself included. My response was a very professional: "Hello, how can I be of assistance and what questions do you have?"

The correspondence escalated to what I like to refer to as "social media bullying" where I was being asked about my upcoming Loki Devotion Class. These kinds of attacks happen all too often. In fact, those of you reading this that are not fond of Loki may feel like I am attacking you. Again, this is merely my devotion and my journey, so take from it what you want. In my professional work as a full-time priestess, there is an art to handling social media attacks and that art really consists of refusing to engage. But, as stated previously, I am a Scorpio and choosing to not engage is just not something I do. So I let this person go off on how I was inviting an "oathbreaker and mischief-maker" into a space that was supposed to be sacred and that they would not be attending.

My response was to explain that the "oathbreaker and mischief-maker" that you loathe so much is the reason you have that hammer around your neck. So maybe you should take it off and have a good day.

Loki is the reason, the catalyst and the instigator into the creation of Thor's mighty hammer, yet so many MDHs (modern-day Heathens) refuse to give Loki any credit. They wear their hammers with pride and call to mighty Thor for strength and they adamantly reject Loki at their Rites.

SIF'S HAIRCUT AND THE CREATION OF MJOLNIR

Imagine the gods doing their god-like duties, whatever those may be. Sif, being the wife of Thor, is lounging about with her luscious locks of golden hair – her beauty is her power. This lounging about in the sunlight is a bit exhausting, so she falls asleep.

Loki who, for good reason, loves and loathes the gods, stumbles upon Sif in her napping and maybe out of boredom or maybe disdain he decides to cut off those gorgeous gold strands. Catalyst!

This precipitating act of cutting Sif's hair instigates a rage so frightening. With Sif's locks gone, Thor is out for revenge when he sees his now bald bride. Loki, who is always to blame, is seized by Thor who threatens to break every bone in his body. Loki, who has rhyme and reason, pleads with Thor to spare his life and allow him to journey down into the realm of the Dwarves to seek their master crafting in creating a new head of hair for Sif.

Thor agrees and Loki descends and convinces Ivaldi to craft a new head of hair. But Loki doesn't stop there. He also gets Ivaldi to create the best of all ships, Skidbladnir; and Gungnir, the spear. Clever Loki. In the realm of Dwarves, Loki seizes opportunity and begins to do what only Loki can do and that is to play the Dwarves against each other in a battle of craftsmanship.

He begins to entice Sindri and Brokkr to a challenge. Can they out-craft Ivaldi? Loki, being so arrogant, even bets his own head, quite literally. Sindri and Brokkr accept. Here we see Loki activate a counter-play in the guise of shapeshifting. Loki turns himself into a fly and invades the workshop where Sindri and Brokkr are determined to win this bet and kill the infamous Loki.

As a fly, Loki is mischief-maker and god – villain. He bites Brokkr on the neck and eye, which prevents Brokkr from seeing in detail what he was crafting. Needless to say, the Dwarves succeeded. They created three incredible masterpieces.

The first being a boar called Gullinbursti which could run on water or in the skies faster than any horse. The second being the golden ring, Draupnir, from which, on the ninth night of wearing the ring, eight new rings would fall. The third *being a hammer of such incredible quality it would never miss its mark. The only flaw being that the handle was too short; this was thanks to Brokkr's swollen eye not being able to see his work in its entirety.*

Loki returned to Asgard with gifts in hand. To Sif, her new golden hair. To Odin, the spear of Gungnir and the ring, Draupnir. Freyr received the boar, Gullinbursti, and the ship, Skidbladnir. The gods were grateful and their anger at Loki softened ... A bit.

But what about the Dwarves? Well, they won the bet! They went after Loki's head. But here we see Loki as mastermind and the Cunning One – he agrees to give them his head but reminds them that he never agreed to giving them his neck. The Dwarves could not take his head without damaging his neck so they compromised and sewed Loki's mouth shut.

This story makes me laugh so much! All of these events occurred because Loki was bored and felt like creating a bit of mischief when he cut Sif's hair. Imagine what we mere humans could do if we embraced our boredom with creativity?

Thus, we have Loki to thank for the Mjolnirs that we wear and tattoo upon our bodies, not to mention the spear of Odin, the boar and ship of Freyr. Loki as catalyst simply took advantage of time and gave a little push, or rather cut.

Where could you use in your life a little push? A nudge? When you think of anger, it too can be a catalyst. But what fueled the anger? That's a catalyst too! Each day begins as an eruption and each day is filled with catalysts.

Webster's dictionary defines catalyst as: "an agent that provokes or speeds significant change or action." The alarm going off in the morning is a catalyst that provokes you to get out of bed! We have physical catalysts, emotional catalysts and scientific catalysts.

> *"Loki catalyst. He is the mover, the shaker, the one who provokes."*

We are seeing a rise in spiritual leaders who are themselves catalysts that are activating courage by expressing their beliefs openly! Each October, I wear my witch's hat to provoke conversations on what witchcraft is and is not. This is my act as a catalyst in my very patriarchal religious State of Utah. How are you being a catalyst? For whom?

For some, this act of simply wearing a witch's hat is an act of aggression, a violent attack on their sense of normalcy. The power doesn't come from the hat or even me as the wearer. The power comes from the one who reacts or chooses not to react.

With our emotions being triggered by catalysts, we can either activate those reactions by embracing them and thus those reactions become catalysts for altercation, or refuse to engage and focus energy elsewhere. There is an incredible amount of power expressed when one chooses to not engage. That refusal to engage becomes a catalyst for a new kind of shift in awareness.

I fully know that my witch's hat is going to offend people. But I also know that it is going to give those who are still in the broom closet permission to step out a bit. By choosing to wear my hat in October, I am softening the affront because it is socially acceptable to dress up (and not just as a witch) in costume in October.

Think of people in your current life situations that are catalysts. What is it that they do that inspires you or provokes you? How much power are you giving them by reacting or engaging? I could have really dived into the social media attack and spent precious time and energy into defending why I would openly host a Loki Devotion Class. My practice, just like yours, is not open for discussion nor do I feel the need to explain it and nor should you.

As an individual practitioner, my rituals of devotion are mine and I do not answer to the social media police scammers. I don't get out of bed each day and worry about who I am going to offend. We as mere humans have zero control over other people's feelings and reactions. Self accountability is a super power! When you can consciously admit your own choice of feelings you become the catalyst for change within your own life. You do this because you no longer embrace and anchor into victimhood. Victimhood being blaming other people for how you choose to feel. I could have been offended that this person didn't want to come to my events because I openly welcome Loki. I could have been offended that they thought my space wasn't sacred or safe. If I had chosen to react and defend then I would have given over my power to that person and I refuse to do that.

When embracing Loki as catalyst, and in general, it is vital to remember that he is a creature of duality. He is light/dark, good/evil, catalyst/instigator and so forth. He isn't one to swing the pendulum graciously. He is rather like a Gemini – a bit two-faced (sorry to all you Geminis reading this but you know it's true). There is no soft middle ground to sit and be comfortable when working with Loki. Just like a Gemini – there is no soft middle between emotions. A Gemini is either pissed or happy! At least, the one I live with has proven that.

Loki is either pushing you or pulling the rug out from under you. He definitely is NOT sitting next to you, calmly waiting for the storm to pass; he is the bringer of the storm. He dares you to engage or disengage. Loki is intentional manipulation. But you, the individual, cannot use him as a scapegoat. I often hear people who are new to the Craft (myself being guilty of this in my early years) blaming a deity for what is happening in their life.

Once at an event, my high priestess at the time made a statement concerning the tension occurring at the event, saying: "This is all the Morrigan, coming to play." Yes, there was a battle but it was not a deity causing it. The contentious battle was humans embracing their ego and riding their chosen offenses.

Loki doesn't cause things to happen in our lives; we as humans like to attach blame to deities, gods and outside forces, instead of seeing that the power really lies in how we as mere humans are choosing to react to the catalyst forces.

Deity work is really mirror work. We have created attributes that we attach to and connect with deities. That energy and those attributes we see mirrored back to us in our interactions and day-to-day experiences. Do I believe that a powerful goddess like the Morrigan chose to create a battle amongst 33 women at the event? No. I do, however, believe that her energy of battle was being displayed by the attendees.

Do I believe that Loki has been creating chaos in my life this past year plus? No! But maybe. How does one really know?

I do, however, personally believe that in my process of devotion I have welcomed chaos as a catalyst and so. in my day-to-day experiences and interactions, there has been a bit more chaos than I have consciously chosen to see. At least, through this process of devotion, I am witnessing the chaos more because I am self-aware of what I have asked for and invited. It is now up to me as the individual practitioner of my Craft and master creator of my life to either embrace the chaos that I have asked for or to blame Loki, who may or may not even exist. This blaming or needing a scapegoat or adversary is a pretty common attribute amongst mere humans. There just always has to be a bad guy. Do I see Loki as a bad guy? No! Chaos is not bad. Catalysts are not bad. We need something to propel us forward. This act or incident that triggers us as individuals just enough to want to react is not bad! It is life!

The alarm clock going off in the morning that interrupts our dreams is often the catalyst that prompts us to get out of bed and begin the day. Deadlines at work are catalysts. Emotional woes are inner catalysts that are desperately wanting our attention so that we can feel them, allow them and move through them to create a state of balance.

"Small steps can lead to a big impact, especially when coupled with a catalyst mindset." Babajide Olowookere, in an article published in May of 2023, talks in great detail about embracing a catalyst mindset. He states that being open to change, taking actual steps towards your individual goals and being a constant student of what life is teaching you is recognizing that the smallest changes can lead to big results. He offers some tips to living with a catalyst mindset such as:

1. Set realistic and achievable goals.
2. Be open to trying new things and experimenting with different approaches.

3. Take action every day, no matter how small the task maybe.
4. Make time for personal reflection.
5. Challenge yourself daily.
6. Be persistent and never give up.
7. Believe in yourself.

Let's be honest, life is hard. Chaos is unavoidable and we can shift things by loving the catalysts in our lives, especially those catalysts that we as individuals create. A catalyst mindset means having the ability to realize opportunities. It also involves being open to new experiences and ideas and being willing to let go of the old thinking patterns that no longer serve you.

If you are a card player, you know that if you play the same hand you will always get the same results. When we apply this to our lives we know that if we constantly repeat the same actions each time in a situation (whether that's in handling a dispute with a coworker or healing a disagreement with an intimate partner), we will get the same results. Growth doesn't occur in this state of complacency and using more of the same approach. We have to be willing to try new things for not just ourselves but for the other people involved.

My romantic relationship has been 23 years of chaos fueled by cataclysmic upheavals and spurts of ego that really are giving my lover and I opportunities for exponential growth, both as individuals and as a couple. Do we embrace these? NO! We resist and often play the same cards while simultaneously expecting different outcomes – the results being victimhood, blame and frustration.

As individuals capable of incredible things, it is vital that we move out of comfort and step into the unknown – embracing the unpredictable moments and allowing ourselves a more catalyst mindset to help us move forward and onward.

Grieving the loss of my friend and feeling this new physical dis-ease have been two major personal catalysts this past year. There have been many times that I have not wanted to get out of bed or push through. My mantra has shifted to playing new cards each day and embodying the "I can and I will because I am worthy" attitude. My friend would want me to push through the little hiccups each day. My body needs me to push through! What new card(s) can you play today?

CHAPTER FIVE

Light-Bringer or Devil?

Being born and raised in Utah has its challenges. Utah is a state founded out of desperation to escape religious persecution. The dominant church for decades has been the Latter Day Saints (LDS), also known as the Mormons. Luckily there is a shift occurring and this church no longer is dominant. However, it has done its damage.

As with any structured organized religion, there are problems. Most of these occur within the hierarchy and leaders who represent. The focus of this church is patriarchal control, fueled by fear of a vengeful and jealous God.

Growing up, I was raised in this church. Lucky for me, my parents were not raised in this church, so they already possessed a more open way of viewing religion and the world. With this ideal and threat of disappointing God or Heavenly Father (as the Mormons refer to him), there is another masculine figure that seems to actually get more attention – and no, it is not Jesus, although he does get the spotlight quite often.

This other masculine figure is none other than Lucifer, the Fallen Angel – or rather, the brother of Jesus. Lucifer and Jesus are brothers that are pinned against each other in a very unloving, opposite of family.

For me, I look at them as two sides of one whole – one being light and one being dark – but I will save that for another book. Lucifer is a very misunderstood character, much like Loki. Lucifer too has many names: Satan and the Devil being the two most popular. In Hebrew, the name Satan means "accuser".

In the Mormon Church, Satan is the instigator and the catalyst. He is the tempter, or the "Evil One". Father of Lies. He is the Great Imitator. In the LDS faith, they view Satan as the antagonist and the one whose only goal is to destroy the family. He is the one to blame.

When you actually dive into the discussions and public talks given by leaders of the LDS faith and see all the many things that Satan is responsible for, it is a rather depressing rabbit hole. If Satan is to blame for just about everything then it does make one question whether individuals in this church actually have any resemblance of individuality and self-accountability.

Satan is the master of addictions. So, if you engage with any kind of substance (be that a physical form of consumption or virtual) that is addicting, then you have become addicted because of Satan. You are not even allowed to read this chapter in this book. It is not good practice to become intrigued by Satan and his mysteries. No good can come from getting close to evil. Like playing with fire, it is too easy to get burned. The only safe course is to keep well distanced from the Devil and any of his wicked activities or nefarious practices.

The mischief of devil worship, sorcery, casting spells, witchcraft, voodooism, black magic and all other forms of demonism should be avoided like the plague. Growing up, in Sunday school the majority of classes were focused on Satan – ways to recognize his wicked temptations and reasons to avoid him in order to ensure one's salvation in heaven. They mention him in videos, books and during almost every lesson. For me, that constant focus on Satan is a form of worship.

As a witch and public figure in my community, I often get asked if I worship the Devil. My response is usually to quote Sandra Bullock from the movie *Practical Magic*: "there is no devil in the craft, he is a Christian creation."

This Satan character, who receives the spotlight more than Jesus or God does, is given quite the pedestal and power – much like Loki, who is blamed for everything and who is at the center of everything. The two have undeniable similarities. Lucifer – the name means light-bringer. At least, it did when Lucifer was an angel – a beautiful angel who fell from grace – meaning that he defied God's control and demands. So, in angel-form he is known as Lucifer but once he rejected God he became Satan.

Loki is also known as light-bringer. Coincidence? I think not. With ancient practices being oral in tradition and very little if anything being written down, we have a mix-matching of customs being shared and expressed. It is not uncommon to see similarities amongst gods and goddesses throughout different countries and cultures.

In the Norse myths, which were written by a poet/historian/politician who heavenly (pun intended) incorporated Christian concepts, does it make sense to incorporate an adversary much like the Devil into the sagas of Odin and his nine realms?

The Devil, no longer the angel Lucifer, goes into the Garden of Eden to temp Eve. Why did he supposedly select Eve as his target? Is it because she was vulnerable and not a whole being? After all (according to their creation story), Eve was made from Adam, right? She was not a whole person. Women have been depicted in Christianity from the beginning as the weaker of the sexes. It all began with Eve and her acceptance of the Devil's temptation.

What did he tempt her with? Knowledge. Not just any knowledge but the knowledge between good and evil. In fact, the Devil told Eve: "If you eat from the tree, you will be like God, knowing good and evil."

Now it is my knowledge that the entire scriptures and doctrine of Christianity is focused on becoming like God. So, what did the Devil do? Wasn't he actually helping? If it wasn't for the Devil, Eve and Adam would still be hanging out in the Garden of Eden and humanity never would have happened …

Creation myths are fascinating – and humorous. So Eve was tempted. Not actually by the Devil in the form of man but the form of a snake. We see shapeshifting in action and another similarity. Loki is often represented by two snakes intertwined to form an "S" symbol.

Snake as animal medicine is the creature of rebirth, transformation and creation. It makes sense why the Devil would appear in snake-form. Snakes also represent immortality and the ability to heal and be reborn. Loki has a connection to snakes as he is the father of Jormungandr – which we will discuss in a later chapter.

Norse Mythology, much like Christianity, is filled with stories that are metaphors of how one could and possibly should live one's life. In each, there are main characters – always a golden son and an adversary. What I love is that the Devil character takes main stage in both. Why is this? Why as mere humans do we need a fall-person, a scapegoat and someone to blame?

Scholar, Jerold Frakes, states that: "Loki has attracted more scholarly attention during the past century than perhaps any other figure in Norse mythology, primarily as a result of his ubiquity and importance in the surviving mythological documents and the almost universally acknowledged ambiguity of his character." Like the Devil, Loki is so popular because is not a "fixed" character. He is dualistic in action.

Loki is the good guy and the bad guy simultaneously. He is the villain and the hero. He literally is saving people through his villainous acts – much like the Devil. The Devil saved humanity by giving us choices between good and evil. He gave us his power, yet he is demonized because of it.

Tim Callahan, a poet and artist, shares a similar view: "Just when we've decided he's a villain, he does something heroic. Just when we're sure he's a fool, he does something intelligent … yes, the Trickster does charm us, even when we know he's lying."

According to a census in 2021, Satanism and devil worship is on the rise. In a time of chaos and uncertainty, when traditional belief systems no longer seem to have all the answers, more and more young people are finding comfort in Satanism. The Church of Satan doesn't believe in the Devil nor does it recognize "Satan" as a physical or even a spiritual being. So, why the appeal? Why the increase?

As a manager of an independent bookshop, I get to engage in conversation often. Just the other day, a man came into the shop and he was gazing at our rapidly growing metaphysical section and he asked me if there was a larger than normal community of witches and Pagans in the area. My response was to chuckle, but instead I informed him that Paganism and witchcraft are the fastest growing practices in the world today. More and more people are turning their back on organized Christian religions and embracing other outlets, like Wicca and even Satanism.

The look on his face was pure shock! The small city I live in is very diverse. We are known for the Shakespeare Festival and our university is anchored into theater and the arts. Each year we get an influx of new, hungry students who bring with them a very eclectic energy.

With this customer, I had to explain to him that even though we are in Utah, Mormonism is not the dominant religion in our city. We in fact do have a very large Pagan community. We also have the very first Goddess Temple (which my lover and I built, brick and mortar, back in 2017).

Organized religions have failed our society and this younger generation is really taking notice. Nothing shocks customers more than our copy of *The Satanic Bible* that we have at the shop. We have to reorder constantly as it is one of the bestselling books.

The Satanic Bible, written by Anton LaVey back in 1969, is filled with essays, rituals and observations made by LaVey, who is the founder of the Church of Satan and the religion of Satanism.

When my son had to read out loud a book in his English class, he was uncomfortable and didn't want to do it. He thinks he has a speech impediment and adamantly wanted to skip school on the day he was supposed to read. We as parents encouraged him to be a bit more "clever" and so we ordered him a copy of *The Satanic Bible* at his request. When it came time for him to read out loud, he was conveniently excused from doing so.

People in Utah tend to run in the opposite direction at any mention of the Devil, Satan or witchcraft. My son passed his class and never even had to participate. What happened though was that he read the book and he now proudly refers to himself as a Satanist – maybe for shock factor, maybe not.

The mission of the Satanic Temple (a religious organization) is to encourage benevolence and empathy among all people, reject tyrannical authority, advocate practical common sense, oppose injustice and undertake noble pursuits. There are clear philosophical differences between the Church of Satan founded by LaVey and the Satanic Temple which should be seen and recognized as they are two separate entities. The common ground amongst both is the reference to Satan and self-accountability and responsibility for one's actions in the world and their community.

The Satanic Temple claims to have over 700,000 members and those numbers are rising every day. More and more followers are expressing that the Devil or Satan-figure or character is one of strength and independence, which makes sense and is why more and more people are turning away from Christianity which is becoming a rather outdated modality in today's world of chaos.

While Christianity is focused on fear tactics to gain control over members, Satanists are conquering their own fears and holding themselves accountable for their actions rather than placing blame on an adversary for the choices they themselves make. Christianity is more exclusive, while Satanism is inclusive.

Body autonomy and rights over one's own body have come under attack recently. This has increased the number of people turning away from the control of mainstream religions and embracing Satanism, Paganism and witchcraft. Luciferianism (which is a branch on the tree of Satanism) is focused on the positive aspects of Lucifer.

If Lucifer means "bright star", "morning star", "shining star" and, again, "light-bringer", then one could naturally assume he was a deity, angel or god of goodness. Luciferian teachings can be found in Masonic, Wiccan and New Age concepts – there is no actual dogma or established church. Most Luciferians see themselves as gods of their own lives. They are focused on living in a good and loving way, being seekers of knowledge and opening their minds to a higher way of thinking. There is no worship of Lucifer amongst Luciferianism. Just like there is no worship of the Devil in Satanism. Both honor the attributes and actions of Lucifer and the Devil. Even in Wicca, practitioners are not worshiping deities.

Individuals are simply seeing enlightened qualities and attributes in these figures and striving to live in a complimentary manner. When we look at Loki, we see an icon of independence, a stereotypical bad guy and one who is gender-fluid. When we look at Satan, we see the same.

When we look at Lucifer, we see beauty, knowledge and goodness. We see two figures that have been hated for centuries because of their unwillingness to conform. We see two figures that were hungry for answers, so they questioned the norm and rather than embrace the comfort of being a blind follower they were willing to tempt fate, poke the bear and push against the rules being imposed. They dared to be both good and bad. They dared.

PRINCIPLES OF LUCIFERIANS ARE:

- Seek knowledge.
- Ignorance leads to hatred.
- Each person is responsible for their own fate.
- Strive for success and enjoy the fruit of one's labors.
- Delight in the so-called pleasures of the flesh.
- The behavior of others dictates how they are treated.
- Self-determination. Enlightenment is the ultimate goal.

SEVEN TENETS OF THE SATANIC TEMPLE:

- One should strive to act with compassion and empathy toward all creatures in accordance with reason.
- The struggle for justice is an ongoing and necessary pursuit that should prevail over laws and institutions.
- One's body is inviolable, subject to one's own will alone.
- The freedoms of others should be respected, including the freedom to offend.

     To willfully and unjustly encroach upon the freedoms of another is to forgo one's own.
- Beliefs should conform to one's best scientific understanding of the world.

     One should take care never to distort scientific facts to fit one's beliefs.
- People are fallible. If one makes a mistake, one should do one's best to rectify it and resolve any harm that might have been caused.
- Every tenet is a guiding principle designed to inspire nobility in action and thought.
- The spirit of compassion, wisdom and justice should always prevail over the written or spoken word.

Sharing these principles and tenets is a way of shedding light on false perceptions surrounding both practices. With my year plus spent in devotion and studies of Loki, it has become more and more clear that Loki is the hero, he is the bringer of light and he was cast out.

The Devil, Satan, Lucifer and Loki are one and the same. Robert Wheelersburg, who teaches Scandinavian studies, wrote: "Arguably, Satan and Loki were the closest parallel between two religions. Both were semi-divine beings banished from heaven who brought evil and mischief to the mortal world." While Loki doesn't have a religion dedicated to him, it wouldn't surprise me if in the near future a group of people decided to create one.

There is a rumor of people calling themselves "Lokean – someone who worships and works with Loki as the primary deity in their personal practice." This is not factual, rather individuals collectively creating a term to describe their personal devotion. I would liken myself to a Lokean, only I do not embrace the word or action of worship as that is a heavily Christian practice and I am in no way, shape or form Christian.

One can honor the attributes and characteristics of Devil, Satan, Lucifer and Loki and be agnostic, like myself. I do not know for certain if any of them actually existed. All I know is that there is good and bad, duality in each individual and animal on this planet. There are characteristics that I admire and can exercise within my own life and practice.

Maybe I am more of an "agnostic atheist – one who doesn't believe but also doesn't think we can ever know whether a god, devil or Loki exists." Embracing shock factor as a tool has proven to be effective. Clearly, so many people are easily offended and shocked! The mere combination of "Satanic" and "Bible" triggered a chain reaction of knee-jerk cringing; people became both curious and outraged. Either way … success!

Let's face it, we as humans like to be rebellious and when we are taught that Satan, the Devil and Loki attributes/ characteristics and similar characters are to be avoided with no actual reason as to why – we do the opposite. If you remember being a teenager then you can relate. The second a parent said "don't smoke", we did what? Picked up a cigarette.

We are attracted like a magnet to things that we are told we must avoid at all costs. We are taught what we should be offended and repulsed by. We are spoon-fed fear. We mere humans must have an adversary, a dark one to counteract the light. This fear-based thinking, living offended and being triggered serves what?

Hermione Granger said it best: "Call him Voldemort, Harry. Always use the proper name for things. Fear of a name only increases fear of the thing itself." She's not wrong. If we are taught to be afraid of certain characters and their characteristics in myths and legends then we will be afraid of them.

We see this all the time in our modern world where pretty much everything is offensive. Cancel culture is alive and well, to the point that people are living in fear based on not wanting to offend others.

When I changed my name to Gypsy over a decade ago, a small percentage of people were offended, they had been taught that the term gypsy is a racial slur. I was never taught that. Historically, yes it was a derogatory term used to describe an ethnic group of people. Some people unfortunately still use it as a slur today. But gypsy has also been given a resurgence of positive attributes.

Just like the word "witch". While 20 years ago, calling someone a witch was an attack on their character similar to calling them a bitch; back in the 1400s, calling someone a witch was literally a death sentence. Yet what do we see today? Witch is being used in a positive light, rather a form of empowerment and self-proclamation.

We have the choice to give power to words, titles and individuals. Just because one person says that a word is derogatory, doesn't mean that it is to the masses. It is best to engage and ask the individual: "what does that word mean to you?"

Calling someone a "devil" can result in multiple reactions, but those reactions are anchored into the individual and their personal connection to that word. In this world, we are seeing a rise in people claiming their true selves through identification and specification of what their identity is.

It has become socially acceptable for people to change their names, their genders and their roles within society. All of this is good. It highlights individuals claiming their individuality. We don't go around getting mad at people for changing their name to Star or Rainbow. People as individuals have the right to proclaim their individuality. It's rude to attack or question an individual's pronouns and self-identification.

When my mother gave birth to me, she didn't have a name picked out. She was told I was going to be a boy. Before she could take me home, she had to put a name down. So she chose her first name and my dad's middle name. Growing up with both parents' names was a cause of confusion and it was never really my name. As a teenager, I tried on a few different names. It wasn't until I heard the song *Gypsy* by Stevie Nicks and read the words that it all clicked.

Devil worship isn't what it was ten years ago. Reading *The Satanic Bible* is more than okay in a public setting. We as individuals that do not fit into the norm or rather what we thought was the norm in society are stepping out and living boldly.

Amazing!!! Hermione telling Harry to just say Voldemort's name is huge! It lessened the fear. Calling Satan Lucifer is doing the same thing. No one knows if Lucifer/Jesus or Loki/Baldr were good/bad or light/dark. All we have are stories – stories that someone else wrote and attached a good or bad vibe to each character.

As creatures capable of adapting, we as humans need to remember that this world is constantly changing and we are the ones changing it. Myths and legends, while good metaphors for how one can choose to live, are becoming obsolete and outdated.

"Knowledge is not power, it is only potential. Applying that knowledge is power. Understanding why and when to apply that knowledge is wisdom."

– Takeda Shingen

When people come in to get their tarot cards read, one of my favorite responses is the mouth-gaping gasp when the Devil card comes into play. In the 1910 book that accompanies the *Rider Waite Tarot Deck*, the Devil is characterized as: "ravage, violence, vehemence, extraordinary efforts, force, fatality, that which is predestined but is not for this reason evil."

When I look at this card, I see a horned figure that is part-beast and part-human. At his feet there is a couple loosely bound. For me, the Devil is not a character to fear or avoid but one that is displaying a "caution". His horns represent intellect, his wings the ability to take flight. He bears the inverted pentagram or five pointed star upside down (the inverted pentagram which has been tethered to Satanists due to its depiction on their statue of Baphomet which is one of the main symbols of the Church of Satan). This figure sits, literally, his hand raised in the manner of encouraging one to halt.

A good friend of mine and fellow author, Courtney Weber Hoover, writes in her book, *Tarot for One*, that: "Devils are constant in our journeys. They may be competitors or enemies." She goes on to liken the devils in our lives to physical, mental or even emotional illnesses, stating that: "No matter what their identity, a devil must be defeated, or at least placated, if we are to persevere and complete the journey we've started."

When the Devil appears in a tarot reading, and once the gasping has stopped, further inquiries come into play. I often ask the querent (or person getting their cards read), who is the Devil in their situation and do they feel bound or tethered to this situation? Oftentimes, the Devil comes into play because a person has allowed themselves to formulate a tether, whether that is an energetic, mental or physical tie or bind to an illness, relationship or a situation. The power of the Devil instigates that the individual has a choice. A choice to either break the bonds that the individual has allowed to bind them or to push pause/stop and make steps to prevent the binds from becoming constrictive.

Following blindly the masses no longer works. We have learned to question. We have learned to push against the norm. We are rebellious and, let's face it, we don't like to be told what to do, how to live, what to eat, what to call ourselves and how to live. It's safe to say that Eve wasn't the only one who ate the fruit from the tree of knowledge. Some of us choose to eat it every day.

"Be careful when you cast out your demons (or devil) that you don't throw away the best of yourself."

– Friedrich Nietzsche

CHAPTER SIX

Fire-Starter

There is a bit of confusion when it comes to Loki as being a fire god – confusion or debate.

Again, who really knows? No one. The confusion comes from the similarities in names. Logi, who is also one of the Giants, is said to be the Ruler of Fire. Logi translates into fire, flame or blaze – but again, no one knows any facts.

Who was this Logi character? Well, he's not really mentioned more than once and that is in *The Prose Edda*. But there are many people (mostly in the internet world) who want to jump on a bandwagon of what is and what is not fact. So, this debate of Loki and Logi is unfortunately just that.

WHO CAN EAT THE MOST?

It was not uncommon for Loki and Thor to go on grand adventures. One such adventure brought them into the realm of Utgard, a strange land filled with strange happenings. While there, they stumbled upon an eating contest. Loki, known for his voracious appetite, decided to make a wager against Logi to see who could eat the most meat that was piled onto plates upon a large wooden table.

Whoever cleaned their plate first would be the winner.

With no hesitation, Loki consumed the plate rather quickly. While Logi ate not just the meat but also the plate and the table. In response, Loki expressed that Logi must be a wildfire because he consumes all in his path.

That's the story. The whole story. Now scholars and internet junkies debate away. For me, I personally liken Loki himself to being the spark that ignites a wildfire. His role as catalyst and instigator really gets things moving. He is an annoyance and frustration.

Fire is destruction and chaos – both of which are Loki. He erupts into the myths with no real creation story. He is just there, fully ablaze in all his irritating glory. He burns so bright that he is hated and cast out, much like the fallen angel Lucifer. Loki for me is untamable.

If you have ever participated in a fire ceremony or high magick with a bonfire in the center then you know how unpredictable that fire is. It doesn't matter how much preparation and planning goes into creating that ceremony. Fire cannot be controlled. Loki cannot be controlled.

When I attended my first Goddess Festival back in 2015, I had no idea what to expect. I was a happy, naïve solitary witch and had never experienced ceremonial group magick. The first night, 200 women gathered in a circle. In the center of that circle was a stone fire pit, stacked with wood. I remember the crowd singing as the procession of priestesses came down the steps in the lower circle and began to move in a graceful sway around the stones. One priestess carried a torch to light the fire. There was silence in the crowd. A tiny spark from the torch to the stack of wood began to ignite – but another priestess stepped forward and the other priestesses stepped back. She stood poised, with a gourd rattle in her hand and, from where I was sitting, she was engaging in a conversation with the fire. She slowly began to shake the rattle and as she did so the fire burst up and the bonfire was ablaze!

This was my first introduction to fire magick. Fire is a force. In the world of the elements, fire is the element created. Imagine yourself back in the Stone Age where the first blaze erupted. The awe! "Man make fire!" There is a reason we as mere humans are drawn to fire. It is not only incredibly necessary but it allows us to play gods for just a moment.

Here we get to take small tangible items from nature and create a blazing heat to cook our foods and warm our cold bodies. Plenty of preparation goes into getting one's homestead ready for the cold of winter. As one who has relied upon a wood-burning stove as the only source of heat for the past 20 years, I can testify to this. Just last week, my Lover and I drove the old truck up to the mountain to look for trees to gather for our winter fuel. While my Lover ran the chainsaw, I tended to gather rocks, branches and pinecones (I just played!) – there was a sense of urgency to be prepared.

No one really knows when that first blast of winter chill and snow will hit. Just last year, it hit early and we were for the first time very unprepared. We had to buy wood instead of gathering, but this year we have other goals, we will be prepared. When we arrive home with our truck-load of wood, there is more prep to be done. This was just the fun part, the gathering and play on the mountain.

As one who prefers old school methods and steering clear of modern conveniences, I have opted out of using the wood splitter and instead I've been using an eight-pound ax to split each log. Not an easy task, but determination is overpowering. My goal this season has been to split with the ax three wheelbarrow-loads of wood, five days a week. This is challenging but very rewarding, especially as a female in today's society.

My motivation has been to find that inner spark of force within myself each time I pick up that ax – my inner fire.

Loki is relentless. I too want to be relentless. After all, I have welcomed the chaos of life, so chopping and stacking wood is my inner battle with chaos. Society tells me to take the easy route and use the splitter – after all, it would be quicker and I could split more in less time than it would take for me to chop my three wheelbarrow-loads – but I am stubborn and I set a goal, so I'm going to push through.

Fire is a good catalyst for increasing warmth in one's physical home and instigating warmth within one's soul. When I accomplish a task, I feel energetically warm and fulfilled, much like if I was sitting in front of a fire in our stove. There is a satisfaction that comes from a job fulfilled.

In mythology, fire is rebirth and renewal. A wildfire by definition is: "A large, destructive fire that spreads quickly over woodland or brush." Each year that we experience fire season, we know that the forest is going to ignite – whether that be by negligence or lightening.

A wildfire will erupt like a birth of destruction and eradicate all in its path. We watch the skies anxiously for signs of smoke in the air and hope that the firefighters can catch it in time and prevent it from destroying homes and too much precious land.

This year, the National Interagency Fire Center statistics show that as of 7th November, 2023, there have been 48,681 fires that have burned more than 2.54 million acres! In Utah, we have had fewer than 800 this year, contributing to 18,000 acres destroyed.

Wildfires are a natural part of many landscapes, and several species have evolved to withstand and even rely upon wildfires. In many ecosystems, wildfires are Nature's way of regenerating the earth, allowing important nutrients to re-enter the soil, and creating new habitats for plants and animals to thrive.

When we look at Loki as the force of a wildfire, we are literally inviting a drastic, dramatic force to disrupt or erupt our day-to-day norm and bring in chaos. Again, chaos is unavoidable. Whether one decides to welcome the essence of Loki's destruction is, however, a choice.

When I consciously invited Loki energetic attributes into my life, chaos came and is still surfacing every day. The only difference has been my perspective. After many visits to doctors to figure out my boat days, I decided that this disorder or disability (Mal de Debarquement) can be managed. Most specialists have stated that this disability can be lifelong or it can disappear as suddenly as it arrived. I viewed it as my own personal chaos and began to figure out ways to manage my reactions to the constant sway.

Shifting perspective is vital to everything! The only medication offered for this condition is motion sickness tablets, which for me is not applicable as I do not have any nausea. When I lay down at night on a bad boat day, it feels like I'm swaying on a waterbed. On bad boat days, when I stand still or sit down, I feel like I'm rocking on a boat – in fact, if you look closely, you will see my body swaying.

Movement helped! I also did a spell to disconnect from any fears and medical "worst-case scenarios." For this spell, I turned to Loki and his wildfire.

CANDLE MAGICK WITH "LOKI WILDFIRE"

To activate one's connection with fire, both as a tangible force and internal element, you just need a candle. We all participate in spell-casting and fire magick on our birthdays.

Each year, we light a candle and make a wish, blowing that wish out into the cosmos – this is the basis of fire magic. You can amp up your candle magick by making your own candle, which is a whole new blend of alchemy. Alternatively, you can take an already purchased tapered candle and rub it with oil and then roll that candle in a plate filled with herbs and sacred salts that compliment your intention.

For my spell, I obtained a red candle. This would represent my desire to burn through passionately those fears that I had of never getting off the boat, fears of never being able to travel or walk without a cane – they all needed to go.

For me, red is a powerful color. I took the red candle and anointed it with rosemary oil to remind me of the strength that comes from my ancestors. Then I rolled the candle in dried Echinacea for healing, mugwort for psychic protection, lavender for calm control, peppermint for an abundance of clarity and sea salt for protection.

I then placed my candle in a bowl that was filled with desert sand, fresh mugwort and eggshells – all to help ground and anchor my magick into the tangible realm. I then cast my circle in my own way, called to Loki and asked for his spark to ignite my own inner wildfire of healing that I may be able to shift perspective, burn out and away my fears and reject any medical worst-case scenarios.

I then lit the candle and watched it burn and, as I did so, I wrote down my fears onto pieces of paper and burned them one by one in the flame. Once the candle was completely burned, I sat and gave thanks to Loki Wildfire, as if he was the flame. With my eyes closed, I visualized a large wildfire clearing out and away any residual fears or remnants from my mind and surroundings.

Candle magick is very effective; it combines tangible energy and the element of fire: it is intense. We are seeing more and more practitioners of the Craft posting their candle magick spells on social media platforms. My boat days are every day, but this spell and focused intention to burn away my fears with the help of Loki Wildfire (and yes I am using that as a term and title as it specially states which essence of Loki that I am inviting).

Being clear and concise in inviting certain dualistic and cataclysmic deities is highly encouraged. What has shifted is my awareness. When I am having an intense boat day, I check in with my physical body. Did I get enough sleep? Have I eaten enough protein? Am I dehydrated? These are all things that I can control and if I am depleted in them then it creates a more intense sway.

The main thing is a shift in perspective. When one can look at a wildfire in nature as a beneficial and vital part of an ecosystem's survival then there is less fear and some appreciation, unless of course your house is near the fire.

When one can look at Loki (who is equally as unpredictable and destructive as a wildfire) and allow his essence of chaos to erupt without reaction then there is a drastic shift in one's appreciation. Some storms come into our lives to clear things out rather than destroy – just like some wildfires or situations come into our lives to burn and clear away to allow room for the new.

> "It's all perspective. I spread wildfires everywhere I go. It's a symptomatic quality of being me."

> – Becca Ritchie

Almost every myth and saga features Loki, and what does he do? He spreads wildfires. He is Loki Wildfire.

In late April/early May of 2022, I decided to test my Mal de Debarquement disability and fly to Edinburgh, Scotland, to attend their annual Beltane fires. My intent is to embrace this disability as my own inner wildfire and see if I can push through.

Planning a pilgrimage is always exciting and this time I decided to take my cousin with me. Well, actually, I intended on going alone but my family felt that I most likely would not come back if someone didn't accompany me. One fear I had was that this trip would trigger my symptoms and I would be physically impaired and imbalanced. It felt good to extend an invite.

This trip started out intense asafter four hours on the runway prepared for takeoff, the pilot announced the flight was canceled. Hundreds of people were now stranded in the Las Vegas airport in the middle of the night. My first instinct was to cry, call my Love and go home, canceling the trip.

In these moments of intense chaos, frustration and upheaval, we are as humans ... alone! While I could cry and vent to my Love and share frustrations with other passengers, ultimately I was alone sitting there in the airport, burning up with irritation, stress and soon-to-be regret if I did cancel.

Instead, I took a deep breath and shifted my focus. I had asked for chaos. I knew this pilgrimage was going to have its ups and downs. Travel days are long and intense anyways. What I needed was a safe place to reset. A taxi was called, a cheap hotel checked into and, after some hours spent crying, I booked a seat on the next morning's flight.

Six hours later, I was back in the airport moving through security check-in.

Airports are chaos in the flesh. If you have ever sat in an airport and watched the madness then you understand. Hundreds of thousands of people in lines, running, stressing, drinking, pushing luggage and basically being herded around like cattle in the hopes that each one will reach their destination in time and in one emotional piece. Chaos!

This new flight would give me an hour layover, which is short! But do-able. Other guests that had been stranded the previous night were on the same flight, so there was a sense of companionship and camaraderie. We shared our horrid night's experiences and vowed to make sure we each made it to our final destination. We had formulated a familiar bond.

Well then this flight got delayed! This now left us with a ten-minute window to get from our current gate to our much-needed gate that would take us to London. After some convincing from the flight attendants to our group of fifteen over who should exit the plane first, it was a Hollywood scene that followed. It was deemed that I was the youngest in our group, most fit and I didn't have small children, so I became the runner.

Running through the airport while pushing a carry-on bag is somewhat exciting. Knowing that this run would affect fourteen other people added some pressure. I did my best, weaving through hundreds of people. Activating the power of a wildfire to clear the way before me and giving it my all. When I reached the gate, it was closing, so (in true movie magic) I yelled "WAIT!"

The man at the gate stared at me and simply said "Hey, take a deep breath. How many people are in your party?" When my answer was fourteen he made a call. We were able to make it onto the flight and when I finally sank into my seat – it was pure adrenaline. This travel day was becoming days and I was mentally exhausted.

London airport to me is the worst! Well, except for the pizza. It is not hard to get lost and lose one's calm. After waiting in line, I was told that this flight from London to Edinburgh leaving in one hour would cost me close to 400 pounds. Not going to happen. Once again, I harnessed the burning of emotions and tapped into my intellect and showed this not-so-kind gentleman the email from the initial airline saying that they would cover all accrued costs spent to remedy their error. He handed me a ticket, glared at me and sent me, once again, running.

The minute my feet touched the ground outside the airport at Edinburgh, a calm and sense of accomplishment had made its home within my body. This travel experience that I endured alone was a game changer. It filled me with a passion and appreciation for my inner capability to do hard things. One of the outcomes with this disability is that travel is a trigger and therefore to be avoided. Not being able to travel is just not something I am willing to accept.

I had survived this extreme travel day and was greeted at my flat by my cousin (who booked separate travel accommodations) with a double whiskey. Movement is medicine. A wildfire won't consume without air to propel it forward. After savoring my beverage, putting my bags in the flat and taking a quick shower, we were out the door so I could give my cousin a walking tour of my favorite city.

Our trip was centered on the Beltane fires and when the night came and it was time for us to walk up to Calton Hill, we were two out of 10,000. It was incredible chaos! Brilliant magick! Lucky for us, we were pushed forward to the very front to witness without obstruction the procession of the May Queen.

Intentional fire magick is life-changing. This trip was life-changing. The synchronicities were countless and the element of fire was my teacher every day. Each day, we are gifted with pockets of chaos where we can choose fight or flight with anger or with joy. This trip for me was like seeing a coyote running in front of a wildfire – not to escape or survive but to metaphorically lead the way for the fire to follow.

When the May Queen lit the bonfire at the end of the night, the eruption of 10,000 people cheering was like an explosion of coyotes yipping and yapping with joy and excitement. In all my years of group ritual, this bonfire was by far the largest and most energetically and spiritually fulfilling.

In many ways, this pilgrimage allowed me to be my own fire-starter. I was given opportunities to douse my flames and give up or give in – but I chose not to! Ironically, my disability symptoms were almost nonexistent the entire trip. Maybe it was due to the pure bliss and excitement or maybe my body is balanced when I am participating in things that give me joy and bring a sense of wholeness.

I share this story to highlight how life is always teaching us through chaos. In these moments, hours or days where we feel like a wildfire burning out of control, maybe there is a deeper message in the madness. Maybe coyote or Loki fire-starter is handing us a match and enticing us to light it and burn brightly?

INVOKING LOKI AROUND A BONFIRE

A fire ceremony is powerful and intensely healing. Humans have always been drawn to the flames and not just for heat or cooking our food but for healing. If you have ever sat and watched the flames of a bonfire dance and the only sound you hear is the crackling of the wood burning then you know firsthand just how soothing the flames can be.

This past Yule, we participated in an out-with-the-old burning in our outdoor fire pit. A huge log was placed on the coals and evergreens used to kindle and feed the flame. It was a crackling eruption of flames. The log had what looked like the mouth of a dragon and soon the flames began to spiral towards the inside of the log as if they were burning their way to the center. It was beautiful and chaotic to witness as the flames took over the wood and consumed it.

I poured a bit of oatmeal stout onto the flame and called to Loki to help us activate the burning of all that we no longer wished to weigh us down physically, spiritually and emotionally.

Hail to Loki
Wildfire
Father of Monsters
Lover of the Witch
Brother of Odin
Catalyst of Chaos
Speaker of Truths
He who burns brightly
He who burns away
He who dances around the Fire
Dance with us, wild one
Shout and scream with us
Witness as we release into the flames all that no longer serves us
Laugh with us as we burn them out and away
Help our fire to erupt and consume
Watch as the ashes rise up in celebration
Hail to Loki
Mischief-Maker
Coyote
Hail and Welcome

Releasing things into the fire is a very common practice, whether we do so physically by writing things down on paper or bay leaves, or by speaking them into the flames. There is an elemental power to physically watching things burn.

OFFER UP YOUR FEARS TO LOKI WILDFIRE

Gather some dried bay leaves or small pieces of paper. Write down your fears, worries and insecurities onto the leaves or papers. Build yourself a safe fire within a confined fire circle, or utilize a candle. Call upon Loki and ask him to consume and turn to ashes these things you wish to release. One by one, watch them as they burn. After each leaf or paper burns, take a deep inhale and exhale the ashes out and away.

Meditative burning is also powerful and effective, especially if you are unable to build a fire or light candles. In a meditative space, see yourself as the flame – see your fears, worries and insecurities in front of you and begin to consume and devour each one. Allow your body to become enraged with heat and burn baby, burn.

CHAPTER SEVEN

Kenaz and Laguz

When working in devotion to any of the Norse pantheon, utilizing runes is a helpful and common practice. While there is no specific rune connected with Loki, there is one that for me has helped to activate that Loki chaos.

> Runes are by definition: "letters of an ancient Germanic alphabet, related to the Roman alphabet"
> - a mark or letter of mysterious or magic significance.
> - small stones, pieces of bone or wood, used as divinatory symbols.

It is believed that runes date back to the second or third century – but again, who really knows. To modern-day Norse Pagans and Heathens, the use of runes is essential. If you want to study the runes further, then I highly recommend Diana Paxson's book, *Taking up the Runes*; or *The Book of Runes*, by Ralph H. Blum.

When working with Loki, some people will utilize the rune Laguz which represents "unseen powers, immersing oneself into the experience of life without needing to evaluate or understand. A rune of deep knowing and self-transformation." This rune is excellent in activation, much like a wildfire (even though it represents water) to cleanse and clear obstacles.

Most people take the "L" of Laguz and connect that to the "L" of Loki. This being really the only solid reason they use Laguz when activating Loki. For most, the use of the rune Kenaz is implemented. Kenaz looks like the "less than" sign from math class. Kenaz is the rune of openings and insight. Activating fire, torching ablaze clarity and burning out and away to really be the wildfire and make way for new beginnings.

Ralph H. Blum calls this the rune of "dispelling darkness that has been shrouding some part of your life. The more light you have, the better you can see what is trivial and outmoded in your own conditioning." Kenaz, like Loki, is a rune of duality. Really though, all runes have duality – just like all individuals. Some people connect this rune to Freya. Having a basic understanding of the runes and trusting one's intuition is key. There is no right or wrong way to practice one's individual Craft.

I use Kenaz as for me it represents opening one's mind through enlightenment. Loki as Light-bringer activates chaos to catalyze enlightenment, and Kenaz amps up that intention. When you break down the word Kenaz in Old English and German, it is interpreted as "knowledge". Common descriptions found in my studies are: activated intuition, insight, understanding, passion, flames, fire, creation, rebirth, torch, creativity, inspiration, energy, vision, fire of life, harnessed power, regeneration, power to create your own energy. Water and fire energy – these combined together equal chaos.

Basically no one really knows what the runes actually represent. How could we? No one here on the planet today was present when the runes were being carved into stones. All we can do is formulate through speculation. *Vogue Scandinavia* has a fun website where you can calculate your birth rune. What they express about Kenaz resonates strongly: "Kenaz is the symbol of intuition. This rune gives clarity in complicated situations. You might not have been aware of the light, but this rune gives you hope that you will soon find a solution."

On the tip of the middle finger of my right hand (which is my finger of leadership and personal power) I have a double Kenaz tattoo pointing towards the fingernail. Every tattoo I have has personal meaning for me. Beneath the double Kenaz (which represents my capability to "create my own reality") I have the rune Teiwaz, which tells me to "get to the point" and asks "what do I want?" Together, these runes remind me to take action and make the most of each chaotic moment of my life. If I remain diligent in my personal activation then I will be victorious!

voguescandinavia.com/learnhowtoreadyourvikingbirth runes

Runes are quite efficient in divination and spell castings.

The candle magick spell shared in a previous chapter would probably have packed an even stronger energetic punch had I taken the time to carve the Kenaz rune upon it. There are countless ways to use runes in one's day-to-day.

Some practitioners do a tarot or oracle reading each day as part of their personal practice. For me, I alternate between tarot and an oracle deck; both of these are switched out seasonally. I have way too many decks and this practice of rotating allows me to spend time with all my decks throughout the calendar year.

While working on this chapter, I pulled my deck of *Rune Oracle Cards* off the altar and flipped open the booklet inside and, of course, it opened on the Kenaz page – synchronicity in action. The image on this particular card is of a bare-chested man holding two torches, one is lit and the other is not. The man is looking up and there is a city in the background. While the image portrays torch, fire and strength and the man is very muscular, there is also an air of youthfulness and excitement in his facial expression, looking up while confidently holding fire in his hand.

"Let's reflect on how the strength of desire becomes part of our life and transforms it." When we hold fire within our hand, what is it we are wanting to illuminate? Sometimes it's a room, so we can see clearer in the dark. Metaphorically though, when working with runes we need to dig a bit deeper and find meaning in the symbols. On the card, this strong man is pictured looking upwards, rather than on the lit torch in his hand. Maybe Kenaz is coming through as a way to remind him to stop outsourcing and look for light in others and look down at himself and see the light he already possesses.

In the *Viking Oracle Deck*, created by Stacey Demarco, the Kenaz card image is a flaming torch. The torch is a fire-breathing monster. In the booklet accompanying the deck, Stacey writes: "The way forward is illuminated. Be the change you wish to see. Don't just talk – embody your message to the world. No one can know everything, so learn from trusted others or elders. By illuminating our shadows, we understand ourselves and our behaviors more deeply."

"Kenaz is both the torch and the fire of kinship. It is the force that shows us the right way forward for us and reveals to us the knowledge we need to do our best." All of Stacey Demarco's decks and books are worthy of investing in. What I love is her reminder that Kenaz is BOTH the torch and the fire. We can apply this to our own lives and quest to embrace Loki through activation of Kenaz and see that we are the torch; we hold within us the fire to activate insight and knowledge of our own inner and outer chaos.

Seeing ourselves as torches, strong and powerful and remembering that our spark of essence, our very spirit is our fire – we can light up as brightly as we choose and we can harness the power to burn a blaze so intense we become a wildfire.

Remember back to when you were in math class and learning the greater than and less than symbols and you would draw teeth to differentiate between greater than and less than? When I write or inscribe the Kenaz rune, I like to envision those teeth but they are mine and I am the mouth of Kenaz. For me, Kenaz represents my passion to take a bite out of every opportunity that comes my way. I am greater than the obstacles before me and everything behind me is a small dot.

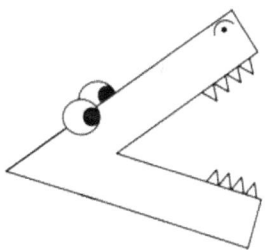

What is in the past stays in the past. Another way to look at Kenaz is to visualize it like the 80s arcade game *Pac-Man*. In the game, you wind through a maze, chomping everything in front of you. Like a wildfire, you destroy what's blocking your progression on your individual path of life. By this destruction of burning or chomping, you are erupting into a transformational rebirth.

If Kenaz is the rune of enlightenment then why do we attach it to Loki who is so loathed and despised? The answer I believe is because Loki possesses an ability to get under everyone's skin. He is mentioned in almost every myth and saga. His tenacity and desire to be chaos sets things into motion. Again, he is the Devil, Lucifer and the Light-Bringer. Our quest for knowing, finding purpose and living fully is our way of searching for a spark in the darkness. Loki is in many ways that spark. He is the trigger – the instigator. The one who pokes those who are complacent out of their comfort zones. He is that itch under your skin that just can't be ignored – at least for some.

For most modern-day Norse Pagans, the Kenaz rune is connected to spiritual enlightenment. A torch or beacon of illumination often precedes personal growth. A spark! When we begin a new journey into the depths of our spirituality, there is usually a spark of interest that leads the way.

As we progress deeper into learning, that spark becomes a torch that brings light and knowledge into our personal practice. This torch burns bright until another spark comes along and we as individuals begin to burn brightly in ways that fulfill us as illuminated beings living our personal truths.

When I stepped back from a solely goddess-only practice to embrace animism, there was a spark. Oftentimes, in discussions about my practice as a Dianic high priestess, I found myself having to defend myself or over-explain my personal practice. It was draining and I felt that misconceptions surrounding the Dianic practice dampened my personal fire. This practice became a box of how-to's and what-not-to-do's. It was constricting and I couldn't breathe. My fire was going out. The spark that first ignited and pulled me out of the confinement of a patriarchal religion and filled me with feminine roar was stifling.

The stereotypical views that Dianic witches were man-haters and TERFs (trans-exclusionary radical feminists) of other modern-day Pagans was not at all what being Dianic meant for me. I had to sit with my own fire and reassess some things. Did excluding men from my circles feel like balance? No! It felt like control all over again.

As one who is constantly searching for and adding sparked logs to my inner fire of knowledge, I kept searching. What I discovered was that there was no one way, tradition or path for me. Rather, embracing chaos as teacher and allowing the rune Kenaz to open not just one door but many at the same time gave me the answers, spark and ignition to move into enlightenment as I choose to define it.

Disconnecting from organized religion was a huge step! I thought that I had done that already when I left the Mormon Church, but Wicca is also an organized religion and felt constricting. When I began to see each day as an open doorway to enlightenment, my entire fire and passion for living fully erupted! Not only was I embracing the rune Kenaz – I was embodying it! Complacency is not home for me.

I am not sure if it is the Scorpio in me or the rebel, but I do not like floating along on the surface. For me, I need to dive into the uncomfortable depths and, once I am there, completely uncomfortable, I must go a bit deeper. It can be rather annoying I'm sure, for those who live with me. But, for me, I need chaos – I need to search, pull apart and push against the barriers.

Rune divination is quite effective in helping in my personal quest to quite literally take a bite out of each day. For me, Kenaz is the alligator that chomps the obstacles that I have placed in my own path. Most of those obstacles are insecurities and self-doubts; although on some occasions what I need to chomp is old ideals that are not really mine but rather societies. As a woman, my challenges are different. As a woman who lives in Utah, these obstacles are enormous compared to women who live in California.

In Utah, a woman's place is in the home – pregnant, multiplying and replenishing the earth. At least that's what the Mormon Church taught. Is it any wonder then why I left that religion and embraced a goddess-only feminist tradition? No! As mere humans, we like to swing the pendulum of life in drastic polar opposites.

Activate achievement through Kenaz rune divination; focus on the image of the Kenaz rune. Can you see its teeth? Maybe draw some to help with the following visualization.

The Kenaz rune gives you the teeth or a spark to ignite and destroy or chew up and spit out the obstacles in your way or burn them clear like a wildfire. Use the bullet points below to write down the five dominant obstacles in your path. The magick is in the details! Be specific; spell-work is about spelling out in detail what it is you are wanting to achieve.

Spend some time and really write down the "what", "who" and "why" of these obstacles in your path.

While you are writing them down, honor the fact that you helped put them there. This is huge!

-
-
-
-
-

Now that you have some obstacles written down, I want you to create space – cast a circle or energetic container in your own way. Light a candle that you have inscribed with the Kenaz rune.

Focus on your breath and your intention. Close your eyes and slowly begin to chant (either out loud or to yourself) "Ken-az" over and over again. Do this until you feel the outside world dissipate and you enter into the realm of meditation where your imagination opens the doorway to possibilities.

Once your chanting has shifted the energy, activate visualization. See yourself as the rune of Kenaz. See yourself as the alligator with teeth or the sparked torch that ignites a wildfire. Become Kenaz.

Now see the obstacles before you and begin to destroy them, chomp them and burn them out of your way. While you are doing this, really visualize all the details of how you will accomplish this removal of them. Move through each obstacle, one by one, until you are done.

Then just sit with your cleared pathway and enjoy the enlightenment of knowing that all the obstacles in your path of life can be moved if you just ignite that spark or show some teeth. In the end, one's relationship with rune-work is completely individual. Anyone can read a book and absorb the author's interpretation – the results are achieved when one utilizes the runes in their own workings in their own way.

Loki is a character of duality, so it makes sense to honor the duality of rune divination to embody and invite that unpredictable energy. We know that calling up the element of fire creates major unpredictable and untamed change. When we balance that fire energy out with water (an element that also instigates and is a catalyst for change) we amplify this energy tremendously.

The rune Laguz is said to be the "flowing waters of creation, consciousness and memory." While on pilgrimage in Scotland, we spent three days in Inverness. When visiting Scotland, one has to understand that rain is simply part of the experience. In November, one can and should expect much more rain – much, much more. Inverness has a loch or river that runs directly through the center of the city. It is an incredible sight and the otherworldly vibe is intense.

One day, we decided to embrace the element of water. After all, there was no escaping it and spending the day in a hotel in Scotland because of a wee bit of rainfall seemed silly. We put on our scarves and waterproof coats and decided to do a five mile trek to where the river meets the sea. It was chilly but with scenery as lovely as we were experiencing, the little bit of cold didn't bother us.

The spot where the river or loch crashed into the sea was absolutely breathtaking. The tiny outlet was grass-covered and all was calm – all but the water. You could see waves slowly (yet with force) colliding with the gentle rocking of the loch. It was mesmerizing to watch the two distinct bodies of water meet each other.

Water is a force. Just like fire – it is untamable and wild. While we stood and watched the loch and sea dance their collision, there were no words that could adequately describe the energy of what we were observing. It was elemental magic – two drastically different waters, yet the same element.

Laguz, the rune of water, contains all the elements of water – the mysterious, unseen powers that shape and yet connect us all. Water is fluid. It ebbs and flows in high tides, low tides, calm waves and tumultuous waves. Water is all around us – the constant blood that flows within us. We go to water to heal, reset, wash away and create anew.

Our very existence began in the waters of our mother's womb. It makes sense that on bad days water becomes a refuge. Waters have shaped our landscape, quite literally moving mountains. Water is unpredictable and is an element to be deeply respected – just like fire.

We rely upon water to douse the wild flames. Energetically, when things get too hot in our psyche, we reach for water to cool us off. We embrace the attitude of "going with the flow" to simmer the flames down a bit. When chaos erupts within me in a state of anger, it can feel like a wildfire burning out of control. Anything and anyone that gets in my way while in this state faces destruction. Oftentimes, I do a quick check-in and ask myself if this inner rage is worth the end result. For me, placing a hand upon my heart and checking-in with my inner water – my blood pulls me out of that hostile state of overreacting and gives me a brief reset. Water both physically and internally brings the rage into balance.

Looking at Loki as water, we can see him as the riptide. While swimming in the ocean just outside of Portland, Oregon, I was taken out by a riptide. Knocked and rolled about with the waves, while my body crashed upon the sand. When I finally was able to surface, I was in a shambles – my swimsuit torn, my hip and side bright red from where it hit the sand with such a violent force I was unsure if I would be sucked into the depths of the ocean, yet thankfully was thrust upon the beach.

Water took me out. It was chaos, unable to be controlled. The only way to really withstand the roar of a riptide is to try to swim to the side and escape the pull, but even then that takes an immense attitude of surrender.

Loki as riptide tests us to see if we will surrender to the unknown chaos of the moment or fight to swim away from it. Like fire, Loki Riptide is wild! With Kenaz as the torch rune that lights the way, Laguz is the rune that challenges one to sink or swim. Can you go with the flow of the chaos or do you need to swim to calmer waters, regroup and then take action?

While opening up the tiny book that comes with my rune deck, I synchronistically opened up the Laguz page. This particular author/artist/creator of the deck refers to Laguz as: "The rune of imagination & inspiration." Can you imagine being faced with a situation where you don't access or tap into your imaginative mind to create a new scenario? We use our imagination all the time! We are constantly in a state of re-imagining our lives to be more. We seek inspiration because deep down we know that there is more out there for us to be, see and to experience.

Loki as Laguz and riptide may use forceful waves to shift us into activating new perspectives, forcing us to choose to react for our own good, for our own survival, or to disengage. For some, Laguz activates "empathy and increases understanding of ourselves and others." I believe Loki does the same.

These past thirteen months, while working with Loki, utilizing the Kenaz and Laguz rune, my empathy for myself and others has expanded. The chaos of emotions expressed in those around me is seen as a flowing river or crashing waves. There is much more allowance, awe and respect as those I care about express their chaos outwardly for me to witness. There is a power and profound love that occurs when chaos is seen with acceptance, rather than resisted.

When a river is flowing or waves are crashing, no person can stop that movement of the water – at least, not physically. Yet when our emotions are flowing or crashing, we do have the power to calm that inner flow and redirect the intensity. We can harness that power within ourselves.

Diana Paxson describes working with runes not only for divination but for healing and defense magic. As an herbalist, I am an avid tea drinker. One way I utilize the Laguz rune is by chanting it over a healing tea, or by making the shape of the rune while stirring the tea. Oftentimes, I call upon Loki to assist me in activating the power of Laguz while I stir my healing teas. Each sip is then a ritual of knowing the chaos in my body has a purpose and Laguz will assist me in shifting that chaos to activate healing.

LOKI TEA

Equal parts of:
- ginger root
- licorice root
- mint
- nettle

A pinch of:
- whole cloves
- star anise
- mugwort

Combine all ingredients, cover with boiling water, let sit for ten minutes then strain and sip.

"Loki riptide, instigator of change and bringer of chaos, stir this water with me and activate it with the healing rune of Laguz.
Help me to embrace the healing powers of these herbs.
Help me to taste the torch of my own creation."

CHAPTER EIGHT

Oathbreaker

Instead of oathbreaker, this chapter should really be titled: *Oh the arrogance and entitlement of mere humans!* Why, you may ask? Loki has a bad reputation for some modern-day Pagan practitioners, or rather Heathens as they typically prefer to call themselves. In these modern circles where a revival and resurgence of the Heathen ways are taking the forefront, it is a common belief that Loki doesn't simply possess a bad reputation – he IS bad! Therefore, anyone who looks at Loki, calls to Loki, respects Loki or sees Loki in any kind of positive light is not allowed or welcome. We can safely say that mainstream Heathenry has a not so welcome opinion of Loki.

In my personal practice as a ceremonial priestess and one who offers my rituals to the public, I have had people openly refuse to attend events because they have seen that I do in fact offer a *Loki Activation Rite* once a year. Just the thought or audacity of me viewing Loki in a positive light has given some individuals the opinion that everything I do must be bad because I see Loki in a different light than they do. Loki has become the Voldemort to many – he whose name must not be spoken.

This baffles me. Exclusion is an unnecessary form of violence. I read a fabulous article on the *polytheist.com* website that offers this insight: *"Oaths are not thrown around liberally in most modern Heathen circles, making an oath is perceived as tying your destiny, your luck/personal power, and your honor to your worth. If anyone else is present for your oath, it is widely believed that their luck and honor is on the line as well, since they are expected to help you uphold your word. Making an oath to a god is tying your destiny, your future, and your life to them, for good or for ill. People who break their oaths are highly looked down upon in modern Heathenry, and some might go so far as to say that oathbreakers have no place in the community, or are even cursed. Some believe that if you break your oath to a god for any reason, they may decide to exact their own recompense from you at their own discretion and potentially from anyone who witnessed the oath but didn't hold you to your word."*

Now I don't know about you, but when I read this, I get a bad taste in my mouth. Almost as if I am sitting in Sunday school listening to a sermon. I get very heavy Christian vibes of control through fear and retribution. Who is holding who accountable? And why do we feel we have that right to exert control over someone and, again, why do we feel that threats have to be established in order for anyone to keep the oath(s) that they made?

Let's step back a bit, what is an oath? If we go by the dictionary definition, an oath is: "A solemn promise, often invoking a divine witness, regarding one's future action or behavior."

If an oath is a promise made, then the only one that can really ensure that promise is fulfilled to completion is the one who makes the promise. No outside person can fulfill another's oath or promise. However, from this we can gather that those who witness the oath being made are therefore bound to ensure the individual keeps their promise or they will face retribution, which could be exclusion from the circle, being no longer welcome to attend circles – or the gods themselves will smite them. Yup! Sounds pretty Christian inspired.

Growing up in a Christian home, the threats of hell and outer damnation were very real – but they were just threats. God has yet to appear to me and thrust me down into darkness because I drank some wine and didn't go to church on Sunday. I realize that, in writing this, I may sound a bit like an atheist but over the years my ideals, beliefs and experiences have shifted and I no longer feel bound by a deity or outside force (other than my own higher power) to hold me accountable. If I have a bad day, that is on me and my reactions, not some deity on a cloud somewhere.

Worship of any of the old gods is not something I promote, nor something I do in my own personal practice. It is my belief that the old gods, like myths, are mirrors that offer us insight of what we as humans can obtain and aspire to be. We as individuals hold ourselves accountable – at least, we should.

Again, we have been programmed to project blame onto others. In this case, Loki supposedly broke an oath to Odin. I don't know if that's true as I was not there to witness it. It is hearsay, which we know won't even hold up in a court of law. But an oath was broken, so now a choice few mere humans feel entitled to exclude from their circles not just Loki but anyone who dares to say his name. Wow!

Loki, a mythical figure given god-like attributes (by us humans) who may or may not have had any kind of factual existence in this human mortal world, breaking an oath with another mythical figure or character who was, once again, given the title of a god and given god-like attributes (by us humans) – having their own existence in their own worlds (nine worlds, to be exact), having their own disputes, their own battles, their own breaking of oaths.

Who are we as humans to think we are entitled to hold not just each other accountable, but we think we have the right to hold and demand retribution for a god (or gods) for something they did in a myth or saga – again, with no actual proof? It's almost comical. We give these figures god-like energy and presence – it's not the other way around. They don't miraculously appear from their other worlds and demand that we worship them. At least, I have never heard of anything actually being documented that states that any of the old gods demanded that humans worship them. We as humans created deities.

These Nordic myths and sagas were written some 200 years later by a supposed Christian historian. They were not based on facts – they were based on oral tradition. If you have ever played the "secret" game where you sit in a circle and one person whispers a secret and that secret is whispered from person to person until reaching the last person then you know that oral traditions are not factual and that those "secrets" are often mis-stated. Oftentimes at the end of the game, the final secret has no resemblance to the actual secret. How do we know what really happened with Odin and Loki?

Loki never broke an oath with me; he never broke an oath with you. He may have broken an oath with Odin but what does that have to do with me? What does that have to do with you? I have met people that won't even say his name, like it is poison on their tongue. Maybe they will be smitten down just by speaking his name, not sure who will do the smiting? It all seems so asinine, stupid and foolish to spend so much time and energy hating, dismissing and excluding someone who is a character from myths and sagas.

We all know how it feels to break a promise. Yet, we don't always need an outside source to make us feel worse. Our consciousness which is ego-based and societal-programmed can make us feel pretty shitty on our own. One of my favorite things to tell people when asked if I believe in an adversary or devil character is: "No, I don't need to blame anyone if things go wrong in my life. I can fuck up my life pretty good on my own."

Accountability is a super power. When we stop blaming other people for our feelings and our reactions, we can progress quite rapidly. Now can we stop blaming gods? Or no? Are we all so perfect that we can't sit with ourselves and own our mishaps, errors and shortcomings? The power of Loki is that, yes, he may have broken an oath with Odin but doesn't this act humanize him? Isn't there a way for us to relate? Who are we to condemn and hold Loki accountable?

When people refuse to attend my yearly Yule events because I openly work with Loki, it makes me laugh. There is chaos all around us, especially in the holiday season. What are these people afraid of? Are they fearful that Loki will add to the chaos, maybe shed some light on the Festival of Light?

Loki is the "black sheep" of the family, the Voldemort or "he-who-must-not-be-named" figure. But shame on us mere humans for forgetting that we too possess those same attributes. We are creatures of duality. We are imperfectly perfect in our own chaos. We have probably broken more oaths to ourselves than actually to others and still the world turns, the Sun and Moon rise and set each day and we are given the same opportunity to do better or worse. But Odin is not going to smite you down if you mention Loki's name. You may be rudely excused from a patriarchal religious sect, but would that really be the worst thing?

When we look at exclusion as violence, this should shift how we handle our interactions in not just ceremonial circles but in humanity. Not one person on this planet is perfect. We are all fuck-ups. Loki is the ultimate fuck-up and his imperfections are held against him like a weapon. There is not a single man-made god or goddess that does not have human attributes of imperfection. Loki broke an oath, so what!

The myths and sagas are metaphors for our chosen realities. We can look at them like the Disney movie, *Brave*: "Legends are lessons, they ring with truths." We see the similarities and the what-not- and what-to-do mirrors. The choice is ours and ours alone as individuals how we choose to internalize them.

Let's look at this oath between Odin and Loki. Mention of this oath comes from *Lokasenna* or *Flyting of Loki,* one of many poems found in *The Poetic Edda* of Old Norse, dating back to 900 and written by Snorri Sturluson: "*Lokasenna* stands out as one of the most vigorous poems of the collection, consisting of Loki's taunts to the assembly of gods and their unsuccessful attempts to get back at him."

Loki spake:
9. "Remember, Othin, | in olden days
   That we both our blood have mixed;
   Then didst thou promise | no ale to pour,
   Unless it were brought for us both."

Othinspake:
10. "Stand forth then, Vithar, | and let the wolf's father
    Find a seat at our feast."

This oath was based on a short passage that reminds the reader that Odin and Loki mixed their blood, which was a common form of swearing an oath. After the blood, it was promised that Odin would drink no mead unless the mead was poured for Loki as well.

What did Odin do when he was reminded of this oath? He demanded that a cup of mead be poured for Loki also. That's it folks! Why do so many people get their panties in a twist? What we see here is that making a blood oath is not a simple promise. Both parties involved in swearing the oath agree to uphold the oath. Odin showed this when he demanded mead be brought for Loki.

Modern-day Heathen practitioners can mellow out a bit and learn from this. If you truly want to honor the old gods, shouldn't you follow Odin's lead and make sure Loki has a seat at the table and a horn full of mead?

As an active high priestess, I have made oaths with members of my then Coven. These oaths were agreed upon by each member so that if these oaths were broken then each individual understood in great detail the consequences that would follow.

When we take on a new job, there is often a thorough job description – we agree to those particular job duties and typically a contract is signed. When we fail to follow through with those duties then there are consequences. This is life, people. We make agreements all the time and we as individuals are accountable for what follows when we choose to break those agreements.

"Cancel culture" and this desire to hold others account-able for things which they have done that do not actually affect us as individuals has become a toxic behavior within our society. When I was asked, rather rudely, why I do a devotional ceremony to Loki, my response was: "Because I want to." When the reply was: "I can't support you or attend your events then," my response was: "Who cares?"

Mere humans are NOT Odin, therefore they do not have the right to impose Odin's consequences onto Loki when in actuality Loki didn't break an oath. He simply reminded Odin of the oath they made together. When one really looks at this oath, it would appear that Odin was the one about to break the oath (not the other way around) and, once reminded of the oath, Odin was quick to remedy the situation.

If you make a promise or swear an oath – then keep it! Or don't – and accept the consequences. This is really the simple lesson behind the Odin and Loki oath. The reality is that Loki is the victim (a term that I loathe). But he is, isn't he? He is mistreated and abused constantly by the Aesir. Yet no one really wants to talk about that. Well, I do!

There is a large group of MDH (modern-day Heathens) who practice the Theodish traditions. This group loathes Loki so much that even the mere mention of his name is not allowed. Theodism began in the 1970s in Northern New York. This particular group has been focused on "rekindling Anglo-Saxon beliefs" through the way they call to the old gods, set their altars and perform their rites.

When it comes to embracing a new path such as Asatru or Heathenism, one should do their research and trust one's gut. There are many self-proclaimed practitioners who do have good intentions and there are many who do not realize what they are representing.

At the end of each day, we face ourselves in the mirror and how we have lived each day as an individual should matter. What we represent outwardly to the public should and does matter. Whether we like it or not, we are impacting and impacted by others. For me, each day begins with an oath to myself to live my day with the utmost compassion and authenticity possible.

Whether you believe that Loki is an oathbreaker who you have the right to hold responsible or not is up to you. Believing dogma based on another person's perspective dismisses your rights as an individual to formulate your own opinion. After all, Odin was adamant that he not be given mead or ale without Loki also being given the same. So, when you are making a grand toast in a blot or rite, remember that Odin thought of Loki as a brother, maybe pour a bit of mead out for Loki and see what happens.

Again, we need to address that most people abhor Loki because he represents chaos – and who wants to welcome that kind of unpredictable energy? In these past thirteen months of intentional interaction with Loki as Chaos, my life has quite literally become a boat on rocky shores, from my friend battling cancer, to travels overseas, to my own eruption of dis-ease and dis-ability within my physical body. My days are worse when I resist the waves of my rocking boat life than when I embrace them with purpose.

Each new wave in our lives is an opportunity to either fight, take flight or surrender. We cannot achieve any of these if we are hyper-focused on spending our precious energy loathing and dismissing a character from myths, sagas and legends who may or may not exist.

"Loki may be a great many distasteful things in the stories; but we are here to write our own story."

CHAPTER NINE

Coyote the Trickster

I had a dream that I was staying at a beach house and there were dolphins out in the water. When I went outside to get a closer look, one of the smaller ones had become beached. I quickly began to slide the young dolphin back into the water when it jumped behind me in coyote-form. The coyote was very large and opened its mouth as if laughing and then it ran off.

Any time I write a book, synchronicity always comes into play. This book has been no different. There are signs and symbols being recognized every day! At least, I am being more consciously aware and allowing them to be seen as symbolic. So, I was not surprised when a shapeshifter came into my dreams.

Coyote in folklore and Native American myths is the Trickster. I wonder if dolphins are the tricksters of the sea? While, for me, I have not found any concrete proof of any of the gods' existence, I have seen a coyote in person on many occasions. There is no denying that coyotes walk amongst us on this planet.

In my first book, *Animals as Gods,* I gifted an entire chapter to the devotion of the coyote. For this book, I want to focus on the similarities between coyotes and chaos. The word "coyote" comes from the Aztec root "coyotl" which translates as "trickster".

These *Canis latrans* are native to North American, from the natural areas to the suburbs. Coyotes are pretty common. They are like ravens of the ground. They are scavengers, mischief-makers and deemed a nuisance.

In the past year, I have personally known two people who have had their small dogs killed by coyotes; one living in Las Vegas and the other in Los Angeles. Where I live, there is an active coyote hunt with no limit on how many coyotes you can hunt and kill. There is even a bounty of $50 per coyote. This is all a supposed act of predator control. In mythology, the coyote is connected to a few deities, the Aztec god "Huehuecoyotyl" for example, who is known for music, dance and mischief. The Native tribes of Navajo, Hopi, Pueblo and Apache viewed Coyote as an anthropomorphic being (an animal possessing human qualities) of creativity, magic, ingenuity, curiosity and mischievous behavior. Looking at Loki, we can clearly see the similarities.

Loki Coyote is a trickster and shapeshifter. When we look back at the myths and sagas, we see a character that is often bored and wanting to push or tempt fate by being the catalyst. Coyote, Loki and Chaos exude cunning perspective and unpredictable actions. They are neither good nor bad – they are whole within their present states.

In the children's book, *Coyote Places the Stars*, by Harriet Peck Taylor (which is a retelling of a Wasco Indian story) a coyote is searching for the secrets of the heavens. He was very skilled with a bow and arrow, which he began to shoot up into the sky. He shot so many arrows that they began to form a ladder which he began to climb. This ladder made it all the way to the Moon. Being curious, Coyote began to shoot at the stars to see if they could be moved. Coyote was successful and soon became artist. He would shoot the stars into the shapes of his friends: Bear, Wolf, Raven and Lizard. He was joyful and wanted to share his creations, so he climbed down from the Moon and began to yip and howl, inviting all the animals to come and see how he had created their image in the stars of the heavens. All the animals rejoiced and delighted in Coyote's clever creations.

This story is so amazing and it really highlights how Coyote was pivotal in his role of being one of the creators.

He was esteemed and respected. Again, this is a myth and Native legend. But like all legends and stories, there are truths and lessons.

How and why did Coyote become an antagonist? A bad guy? Well, humans are responsible for that. Mostly ranchers and anyone who relied upon livestock for their survival deemed the coyote a nuisance. We forget that the early humans invaded Coyote's land and took it for themselves, building fences and introducing cattle and sheep.

Growing up, I always saw the Native tribes of America as the victims of arrogant white people. Maybe this is because my best friend was Navajo and I witnessed a tremendous difference in how she and her family were treated in comparison to myself. Her stories from her childhood were filled with what I deemed magic.

The Native Peoples looked to the plants and animals as the teachers and gods. It inspired me and still does – my friend still inspires me to this day. We can learn from the myths and stories. What if we shifted our perspective from Coyote the Nuisance to Coyote the Artist of the Constellations? Would we be able to shift our relationship to our own inner constellations?

What if we looked at Loki as a catalyst of creative chaos, rather than trickster and oathbreaker/traitor? In looking at the myths and legends, it is vital to see the lessons in the dualities offered and be able to formulate our own inner perspective on those to create our own definitions. We as humans have advanced far too much to simply rely upon the words of others to create our experiences and interactions.

There are believed to be 42 animal-shaped constellations in the night sky. These include bear, eagle, giraffe, lizard, lion, wolf, hare, fox and unicorn, to name just a few – but who put them there? Who named them? We have come to accept them as fact but do we really know? No! As humans, we have this incredible desire to seek answers to the unknowable questions. Who created the Earth? How many stars are in the sky? Who is God? Is there a god? We spend the majority of our lives seeking and trying to gain insight, often to the point that we miss out on the present because we are so deeply invested in solving the mysteries of the past.

When I look up into the skies at night, I see stars. I was taught as a child that those shining lights are called stars, by parents who were taught by their parents, who were taught by their parents and so forth. Someone called them stars somewhere in the past. Like you, I was taught the constellations, which are basically bright stars that connect together to create a distinguishable shape in the sky. Who put them there? Why?

Stargazing is something I take for granted. Living in the open High Desert with no street lights and buildings to block my view of the night sky, I am spoiled. But I don't go out and stare up into the cosmos as much as one would think or expect. My relationship with the constellations is simpler. Knowing the myth of Coyote as a constellation artist I will admit has given me more motivation to really go outside at night and appreciate his artwork of devotion to his animal friends.

What if we were to look at the stories of Loki in a different light? Could Loki Coyote become the artist of chaos – a figure who possesses desirable attributes that make us as individuals long to admire his handiwork? We can sympathize with the ranchers, farmers and individuals who have lost livestock and their beloved pets to the coyote, yes! We absolutely should have compassion and empathy, but there is also a beauty of compassion for coyotes that are living on instinct and these humans and their livestock have moved into his backyard. Having an absolute hate or dislike for an animal acting out on its instincts is unfair, but (as mentioned in the previous chapter) we see this behavior being exhibited all the time amongst humans who hate and dislike other individuals for simply being themselves.

The madness stops when we start to see each other, animals and the olds gods as simply beings of duality. These beings, like ourselves, contain both good and bad attributes but we the individuals are the ones who attach that good or bad definition. Perspective is the most powerful tool we possess.

This perspective is gained through knowledge – and knowledge is best obtained through trial and error. Chaos! How can we embrace our own inner Coyote? When looking at the animals as teachers, messengers and even gods we give ourselves the role of students. Have you ever seen a coyote in its natural habitat? The few I have seen are alert, attentive and going about their own business. In fact, the few I have seen didn't even seem to register my presence. They were just openly walking around.

Two Sundays ago, my Love and I went on a jeep ride just up the road to a rock formation that we call the Matterhorn as it reminds us of the ride at Disneyland. When we parked, I felt the presence of Coyote. As we were moving towards the top of the rock formation my Love went one way and I went the other. He immediately saw a female coyote and I missed it! We went up twice more in search of the coyote and finally I got to see her. She was young, her fur bright and shiny.

As an animist priestess, my goal has been to help people see the animals as divine, whole, authentic individuals, living their own existence free from our definitions of them. The best way to learn is to observe. While not everyone has access to a coyote in their backyard, there are simple tools like Youtube and nature TV channels.

When doing research with videos, I like to keep a journal and write down what words are used to describe the actions of the animals. I also like to jot down what stands out to me. For example, while watching Youtube videos on coyotes and larger predators, descriptive words like: resourceful, adaptable, creative, cunning and incredibly ingenious. These are all attributes that I personally would like to enhance within myself and admire in others.

We can look to animals as mirrors of what we are capable of achieving and more. Coyotes are expanding in population due to their ability to adapt to the increase of humans encroaching on their natural habitat. Think of how you have personally adapted and expanded despite others encroaching on you. These encroachments could be expectations, stipulations, outdated dogma and the list could go on and on. In fact, you may find it helpful to your progression to write down all the things that have encroached upon your habitat and see in writing just how much you have adapted.

See on the paper the power of your inner coyote. See your constellations, your artwork of life that you have created. It feels good to honor progress and see just how far your skills of adaptability have taken you. Eliminating the encroachments in our lives is no different than attacking a predator. Oftentimes, our own self-limiting thoughts create the most damage. We quite literally become prey to our thinking.

The power of animals as messengers and gods is that they do not possess ego like we do as humans. Animals rely upon instincts; they don't do list-making, or weigh up the pros and cons – they simply act or retreat. They don't invest hours talking themselves out of something, like we do.

When the wolves were reintroduced to Yellowstone, the coyote population was incredibly large and now it has obviously decreased due to a larger predator bringing about balance. They could act by attempting to fight the encroaching wolves but they have chosen to retreat and expand into other territories as a means of survival.

Looking at your life, how have you chosen to retreat and in what way did that enhance your life? When I chose to explore a career in law enforcement as an Animal Control Officer – which was an extreme choice (hippie should not go cop) to begin with – adapting was my challenge. How do I adapt in an unknown career and hope to create positive change? My goal was to help the animals but in the egocentric world the animals were victims of the humans and each call I went on was a people-problem not an animal-problem. Toss into that equation being the only female officer in the good ol' boys club, and my ability to adapt was no longer based on survival but personal choice.

Did I really want their sexism to encroach on my personal well-being? No! My choice to retreat from that job was, for me, based on survival. No amount of cunningness or ingenuity was going to save me from that toxic environment. Sometimes, it is walking away from things for your own good and well-being which becomes the smartest decision.

Coyote for me is the mirror to play and remember just how intelligent I really am. Leaving law enforcement was the best decision, but those two years spent in law enforcement were vital to my individual progress, making that job experience the best decision as well.

Coyote shows me that there is a lesson in all experiences, and staying inspired by the process is thinking outside the box. Being okay with retreating is not defeat. It's the knowing of what works and doesn't work and being grateful for the knowing.

Coyotes are often referred to as the "barking ones". If you compare wolf to coyote to dog, you will see distinct differences. Rightly so, as they may be in the same canine family but they each have their own distinguishing factors. Wolves have their own dialog and communication styles. Coyotes yip and yowl. Dogs growl, bark and howl in their own unique way as well.

While doing inventory at the bookshop and working tediously through the "collectible" section, I stumbled upon a 1946 children's book written and illustrated by Wilfrid S. Bronson about coyotes. On the very first page, it states that: "A wolf is a very wild kind of dog. And a coyote is a small, very smart kind of wolf. So, a coyote is a very smart kind of wild dog." What an incredible truth.

The children's book goes on to tell the differences between domestic canines, wolves and coyotes. The book is filled with artwork and highlights the authenticity and wildness of coyotes. It has everything from their slanted eyes to their musical howls and using their trickery to escape predators and how they create a caring home for their pups. Now here is a book that gives a positive view of coyotes by embracing their playful aspect.

When I was hosting a three-day and three-night women's weekend, I had rented a cabin just outside of Zion National Park and each night you could hear the coyotes yipping and barking all night long. They were singing! To me, it sounded like they were having a wild celebration – very different from the howls of wolves and the barking of dogs. Falling asleep to the sound of coyotes really added a bit of magic to the weekend. It helped the women step into the elements and appreciate the natural landscape.

Coyotes are often referred to as some of the most vocal canines, along with huskies. What does your unique bark sound like? What are you barking for or about? Communication is vital to our survival and there are times when we are encroached upon that our bark needs to become louder. No one can express your individual needs but you, because you are the only one that knows what those needs are.

Utilizing coyote attributes as a form of medicine for personal healing, one can see why activating the voice of coyote can be essential. If you want something then you have to express that vocally!

Embracing Coyote as a mirror means speaking your truth when you need to, because you can. Loki as catalyst and wildfire pushed the boundaries and often was the one encroaching on others as a way of instigating or inciting them to bark, bite, howl or yip for themselves. I think of that dream where the dolphin became the coyote laughing at me behind my back.

Why does a coyote want my attention? Are there things behind me in my past that I could have retreated from and laughed about later? Yes, of course! Hindsight is an incredible teacher. Maybe Loki Coyote shows us in the myths and sagas more than we initially thought. Maybe he is showing us that we need to laugh more, play more, create more and be our own constellations, our own works of art that reflect who we really are, not what others' opinions have encroached upon us.

Looking at the tarot deck, it would be reasonable to attach Loki/Coyote energy to the card of The Fool. After all, this card is all about new beginnings, taking risks, being bold, cunning and carefree. Thinking back on my dream, I decided to pick up one of the dream books that we sell at the bookshop which I manage. It said that a dream of a dolphin can represent: "harmony, excitement, using communicating skills to obtain what one is seeking, wisdom and emotional intelligence." Dolphins seem to possess very similar characteristics to coyotes. Both are excellent at vocalizing. Both coyotes and dolphins are playful, mischievous and highly intelligent.

Was the dolphin in my dream that shapeshifted into a coyote trying to teach me something? Yes, I can choose to see the lesson and embody it into my consciousness. Dreams are amazing tools that offer great insight. Keeping a dream journal by your bed is an efficient tool in getting to know yourself through your subconscious lens.

One of my favorite Loki stories involves Skadi the Giantess.

HOW TO MAKE A GIANT LAUGH:

Skadi the Mother of Wolves and Goddess of Winter had reasons for wanting to barge into Odin's great hall, interrupt their feast and demand justice for the untimely death of her father.

She was seeking vengeance.

Odin, being wise and wanting to finish his meal, made a wager. He asked Skadi, what would suffice and soften her rage?

Skadi stated that she wanted a husband of her choosing and a good laugh as she hadn't laughed since her father was killed.

These two things would soften her desire to kill everyone in the hall.

Odin agreed and said that she could have her pick of the gods for her husband but based solely on their feet.

He lined up the eligible gods behind a large tapestry and only their feet could be seen.

Skadi selected the most beautiful pair of feet, hoping that they belonged to Balder the Shining One whom she most desired. The feet she selected belonged to Njord the God of the Sea.

A deal was a deal.

Loki is the one who stepped up to ensure the second part of her needs was met.

He knew just what to do.

He took a nearby goat, tied a string around its horns and tied the other end of the rope around his testicles – yes, you read that right.

He then proceeded to smack the goat on the rump causing the goat to buck and kick which resulted in a jerking of the rope which ultimately brought about a high-pitched yelp, yip and screech from Loki. His yelping, yipping and yowling in pain caused the Giantess Skadi to laugh.

Sometimes we need to embrace laughter as the best medicine. Even on difficult days, a good laugh can be pure magic. After all, we as humans often tend to take life too seriously at times. Sometimes, the best way to retreat from something is to find humor. If the big accomplishment of humans is our ability to adapt, then laughter is one incredible way to prove this ability. Next time you find yourself in a spiral of doom and gloom, do something that will make you laugh, watch a funny movie or be the Fool.

Looking back on my life, there were moments when I invested far too much energy engaging in emotional turmoil, rather than letting laughter help me to retreat. Days of anger, frustration and sleepless nights could have been eliminated if I had just laughed at the fact that I was a mere human experiencing a human ego moment.

The coyote in my dream was showing me that there were times in my life when I made things harder than they should've been – that I was capable of shifting. Coyote in the children's story reminds me to look up and see just how vast the cosmos is and how small and tiny my current problems are. If I can just choose a different perspective then I become the art of my choosing. The coyote picture from the 1946 children's book reminds me that in life there will be tumbles and mishaps, but what is important is getting back up and learning to laugh at those mishaps instead of anchoring in them and drowning.

MEDITATION CONNECTION WITH LOKI
COYOTE

Allow yourself five minutes to disengage from the outside world and focus on your breath. Gift yourself a nice deep inhale followed by a slow, releasing exhale. Repeat this conscious breathing for about five breath cycles. Take notice of how your body begins to physically release all tension as you move through this simple process of inhaling and exhaling. If your mind begins to wander then add a count to your breathing. Breathing into the count of four and exhaling to the count of four keeps your brain focused on your breath-work and makes it almost impossible to have a wandering mind.

Closing your eyes and focusing on your breath, give yourself time to tap into your imagination and see yourself sitting in the forest. You may be leaning your back upon a large tree or you may be sitting upon a large boulder, feeling the Sun warming your skin. This is your meditation and your forest, so see it how you choose.

Once you are relaxed in your forest, invite either out loud or in your mind's eye the essence or energy of Loki Coyote to join you. He may appear as animal-form or human or simply an energy. You have invited him, so allow what appears to appear. Welcome with gratitude.

Here with Loki Coyote in the forest, see before you a basket filled with clear sparkling stones. These stones represent your current situation(s), emotions, people involved and reactions attached to what you are currently facing. There are hundreds of stones! Watch as Loki begins to move around you in a playful manner, prancing, jumping and moving in a mischievous way. See as he suddenly takes hold of the basket and runs off into the forest scattering stones as he goes.

The forest begins to sparkle as the sunbeams bounce off the stones on the forest floor. Loki runs in circles, jumps up on boulders and kicks off of trees, all the while scattering the stones. Allow yourself to feel within your body reactions of frustration, irritation and annoyance to surface. Loki brings you the now empty basket and quickly runs off leaving you with a sparkling mess of stones in the forest.

When you are ready, stand up with the basket in your hand and begin to move from stone to stone, choosing to pick some up and leave some on the ground. You find yourself beginning to create patterns with the stones upon the ground. Allowing yourself connection with choices. Choices to hold onto the reactions, people, emotions attached to your current situation, tucking them into your basket or choosing to leave them where they lie. Some though, you decide to toss out and away, while others become part of an elaborate creation upon the ground – some fantastic design for the Sun to sparkle the forest floor with.

When you feel complete and all stones have been sorted or gathered in your choosing, you simply gaze out and admire your new creations. Opening your eyes and feeling a bit different about your current situation.

REFLECTION:

Oftentimes, when we are facing something that we feel is monumentally challenging, a simple disconnect with breath-work and new perspective is all that we need. Loki Coyote as Chaos was only playing in your meditation. Chaos can be playful. Allowing our reactions to the current situation fall or scatter gives us the power of choosing which ones we really want to pick up and act upon – or do we choose to retreat and rearrange the situation as our own constellations? If you feel inclined, take some time and journal your meditation. Can you see with love all your scattered bits?

CHAPTER TEN

Dancing Shapeshifter

It was my intention to complete this book with a Loki rite and/or ceremony. However, when I began to type that chapter, my mind would go blank. How does one create a Chaos Ritual in an actual format? It seemed silly to me. So, I tidied up my other chapters and asked myself if maybe the book was now complete?

NOPE! When I went to stand up, my hip quite literally went out and I was unable to walk. When I finally hobbled, painfully, into my bathroom to soak in some Epsom salts and do a meditative reach out to Loki and his energy of chaos, what I saw was him ripping out the rite chapter that I had begun and tossing it into a small fire. He then began to dance.

Movement is medicine. Our bodies are not meant to be stagnant; they are their own kind of chaos every minute of every day. While in Scotland, I picked up a book by Raynor Winn about her trek along the Southwest Coast with her husband, Moth. The book was inspiring. Here her husband had just been diagnosed with a severe disability; they lost their home and all their money. They were homeless, broke and facing the unknown of an unexpected disease. So, they came to the decision to backpack a 630 mile walk. *The Salt Path* becomes not just one book but three. Each book is equally inspiring and highlights the magic of movement as medicine.

Here was a couple in their late fifties, stripped of everything, who had never backpacked before and they were camping in a tent. The southwest coastline is England's longest footpath and a National Trail. Ray and her husband Moth were walking on uneven ground, in very cold wet weather. They could have sunk into their defeat, stayed in their friend's guest room and Moth could have given in to his disease and his health rapidly declined.

Instead they walked! When I look back on my bad boat days, even when I would be rocking while I was sitting, there were moments where I would cry and want some kind of magic fix to make the swaying that only I was feeling go away. It was difficult for my family to be supportive on the bad days because they could not relate or really understand. Each step I would take would feel like I was walking on a rocking boat. Movement became my medicine. On these bad days, I found that just walking created a natural sway in my movement that tricked my brain into going with the sway rather than resisting.

When my friend was undergoing radiation treatment, I was able to offer a couple of days and be with her so she wasn't alone. She too, found healing (even if only temporary) through movement. We would walk, even if it was just around the parking lot of the terrible hotel she was staying in. She had her stationary cane, as her ability to walk on her own was becoming almost impossible. She pushed through. Her mantra was: "I just have to keep moving."

Shapeshifting in mythology, folklore, stories and legends is the ability to physically transform oneself through unnatural means. This concept or idea of shapeshifting is the oldest form of totemism and shamanism. In my first book, *Animals as Gods*, I discussed in great detail shapeshifting. As an animist priestess, my public ceremonies and personal rituals are heavily centered on animals and the physical abilities they have.

On my bad days of swaying and walking on the rocking boat, I would often get on all fours and call on the strength of the bear. I started adding bear crawls to my daily yoga routine as a way of building more stamina and physical strength. Bears are powerful, sure-footed animals. My friend would hobble with her cane and say that she felt like a baby deer learning how to walk all over again. As mere humans, we have created a bond with animals and we often interchange the way we talk to include this connection we have to animals. We are animals too!

Yoga poses are inspired by the way the ancient people would observe the ways that animals moved. Animal flow yoga is a combination of traditional yoga and primal movement. When I add bear crawls to my daily yoga, I stimulate my brain which is where my disability stems from; my vestibular system creates the sense of balance or imbalance. By doing exercises on all fours along with balance poses, such as standing on one leg like a crane, my brain and body move like an animal to shift my physical and mental status into balance.

Loki is the Master Shapeshifter. He has shifted into a fly, a snake, a salmon, a mare, a flea, other people and even the elements of fire and wind. Loki is the preeminent God of Shapeshifting. There is no limit to what Loki can do or to what he can become. It is safe to say that the only thing that could possibly limit him would be lack of imagination, and we know he is not lacking in that department.

We look to Loki as Master Shapeshifter. We as humans long to harness the powers of the gods in one way or another. We need more in our lives. We need to have control and at the same time we need a scapegoat (animal term used intentionally). When I saw Loki standing in my meditation tossing pages of my book into the flames, I was not surprised. When he shifted and became the flames, I was still not surprised.

Fire is transformational. There are books about rituals taking place around large bonfires, a frenzy of energy would build and the strongest, most brave warriors would awaken their inner bears and wolves – they would shift into Berserkers! The Berserker myths are incredible!

In 2022, I hosted a three-day, three-night Wild Wolf Women's Weekend. On the third night, it is practice to do a high magick ceremony. Trusting source and the collective energy of the group to help me in planning this high magick ceremony meant that there was no outline, no premeditated ceremony. This ceremony would come straight from my gut. We ended up moving our bodies into a frenzy with breathwork and we became Berserkers! Some of the women felt the energy of a wolf, some felt the energy of a bear. Some felt both animals moving through them. It was one of the most powerful ceremonies I have ever participated in.

Our only limit in our lives is our lack of imagination. When doing shapeshifting ceremonies, one does not physically shift like you see in werewolf movies. We shift in our minds. We open ourselves up to the possibility that we too can possess the physical attributes of any animal we are choosing to connect with.

In January of 2023, I was having the worst boat day week! Each day I would go to sleep and feel like I was on a waterbed that was rocking. When I would wake up, the ground would move out from underneath me. It was depressing. At work, I would drop things as my balance was just off! We had a snow storm one of the nights and I needed desperately to get out of my head and jolt my body.

I needed to embrace this chaos I was feeling rather than fight it.

My solution was to move into the calm of the snow and stimulate my nervous system. Accompanied by my son's dog, Gus, we both went out into the snow. I was barefoot and Gus walked beside me in the snow as I trekked from the porch to the front fence. Not a hurried walk, but a slow deliberately paced stroll in about five inches of snow. My Lover and two sons watched from the window asking out loud: "What is she doing?"

When my friend died and grief entered my life as a new form of untamed chaos, there were extreme emotional days. My friend was a mover, a shaker and a game changer. She was also an incredible dancer. Even while going through chemo and attending one of many fundraisers; if there was music, she would be dancing. She might sometimes excuse herself to go throw up but she would come back and dance! On one particular sad day of missing her, I heard her say: "Shake it out!"

With bare feet, I went out on the front lawn with the dogs and started playing the Florence and the Machine song, *Shake it Out*, and I just danced! Shaking, moving and sobbing the entire time. This song has become my battle song on bad days, sad days, boat days and when I need a good kick in the pants days. Dancing has become my shapeshifting. Sometimes, when I am outside I get on all fours like a coyote, wolf or bear. Dancing, digging my paws into the ground, I unleash that primal rage, that guttural sorrow and I just feel the beat move through my body, becoming one in the moment. Movement is medicine.

Somatic or shaking meditation is now becoming popular. Creating an intentional frenzy through movement and breathwork activates the brain where stored and trapped emotions live. This shaking tells the body to release and let go of the trauma that has been held onto. Oftentimes, I will play the *Shake it Out* song while I simply shake my body – quite literally shaking it out!

SHAKE IT OUT BY FLORENCE AND THE MACHINE:

Regrets collect like old friends
Here to relive your darkest moments
I can see no way, I can see no way
And all of the ghouls come out to play

And every demon wants his pound of flesh
But I like to keep some things to myself
I like to keep my issues drawn
It's always darkest before the dawn

And I've been a fool, and I've been blind (I've been blind)
I can never leave the past behind
I can see no way, I can see no way
I'm always dragging that horse around

All of his questions, such a mournful sound
Tonight, I'm gonna bury that horse in the ground
'Cause I like to keep my issues drawn
But it's always darkest before the dawn

Shake it out, shake it out
Shake it out, shake it out, ooh whoa oh

Shake it out, shake it out
Shake it out, shake it out, oh whoa oh
And it's hard to dance with a devil on your back,
so shake him off
Ooh whoa oh

And I am done with my graceless heart
So tonight, I'm gonna cut it out, and then restart
'Cause I like to keep my issues drawn
It's always darkest before the dawn

Shake it out, shake it out
Shake it out, shake it out, ooh whoa oh
Shake it out, shake it out
Shake it out, shake it out, oh whoa oh
And it's hard to dance with a devil on your back, so shake
*   him off*
Ooh whoa oh (shake him off)

And it's hard to dance with a devil on your back (shake it off)
But given half the chance, would I take any of it back?
*   (Shake it off)*
It's a fine romance, but it's left me so undone (shake it off)
It's always darkest before the dawn (shake it off)

Oh whoa oh
Oh whoa oh

And I'm damned if I do, and I'm damned if I don't
So here's to drinks in the dark, at the end of my road
And I'm ready to suffer, and I'm ready to hope
It's a shot in the dark aimed right at my throat

*'Cause looking for heaven, found the devil in me (oh whoa
   oh)*
Looking for heaven, found the devil in me (oh whoa oh)
But what the hell, I'm gonna let it happen
To me, yeah

Shake it out, shake it out
Shake it out, shake it out, ooh whoa oh
Shake it out, shake it out
Shake it out, shake it out, oh whoa oh
*And it's hard to dance with a devil on your back, so shake
   him off*
Oh whoa oh

Shake it out, shake it out
Shake it out, shake it out, ooh whoa oh
Shake it out, shake it out
Shake it out, shake it out, oh whoa oh
*And it's hard to dance with a devil on your back, so shake
   him off*
Oh whoa oh

Dancing through the chaos shifts the energy and moves one into a state of healing. Movement is medicine. Repetition brings conviction. Most of us start off a new calendar year with intentions to move our bodies more, exercise, lose weight and become healthier. These are the most common resolutions. We all know how good we feel physically and mentally the first few weeks of doing more exercise and eating better, but then life comes along and pulls the rug out from under us – we may experience an injury or illness and have to start all over again. Oftentimes, we give up on the resolution altogether at the mere thought.

Each day is a redo. We have opportunities to shift our perspectives and harness the chaos of everyday life and channel it into expansion. It's not easy, but we all possess the capabilities. Shapeshifting as a daily routine has become a constant ally for me this past decade.

When I am moving through my morning yoga flow, the dogs are usually on my mat with me. They do some of the poses with me. Oftentimes, I can take myself deeper into the stretch when I close my eyes, take a couple deep breaths and visualize my body moving similar to how the dogs move. At the end of my day before I go to bed, as I move through my evening yoga flow, I release consciously with my breath the stress and tension that may have hiccupped throughout my day.

To shapeshift, one doesn't have to move through an animal-form. One can merge with the elemental energies or plants. When we stand in tree pose, we are activating the strength of a mighty oak to help us stand tall and, balanced on one leg, we reach our arms out as branches. This is a form of shapeshifting. When Loki became the flame in my meditation, the flame looked to be dancing. When my hip was out, after a nice bath and meditation I danced like I was the flame. I envisioned my body becoming warm like a fire, my hip felt better within minutes.

Loki turned himself into a salmon to escape the wrath of the gods. He embodied a water animal. In some ways, we could look at this metaphor to teach us that we can keep swimming. After all, salmon are known to swim against the current. We could also look at this as: maybe we shouldn't intentionally create havoc; otherwise we could drown in the consequences. The myths as metaphors are there so we can pick them apart and see the lessons from both sides. What is the saying, "every up has a down?"

Life is going to knock us down. There is always going to be some kind of catalyst capable of triggering something. We can be like Loki and become a fly on the wall and observe what is happening before we react, or we can be like a salmon and swim against the current, or we can dance like Coyote and laugh at the mishaps. I choose the latter.

SHAPESHIFTER IT'S TIME TO DANCE

Take a moment and check in with your body. Place a hand upon your heart and your other hand on your center. Focus on your breath and disconnect from ego by closing your eyes and just breathe.

Once you feel yourself becoming more grounded and (most importantly) centered, move your physical body onto all fours. Now with your eyes closed, envision your hands and feet becoming paws, feel your claws reach out and begin to tap them onto the ground beneath you in a rhythmic beat.

Call to Coyote, call to Loki the Master Shapeshifter and breathe his energy into your body.

Allow your body to merge into the wild, primal shape of a coyote and begin to dance. See all the issues of the day as tiny specks on your back and then begin to shake your back. Shake those issues, triggers, emotional devils off your back.

If you feel like standing as a coyote, then do so. Maybe you want to call upon the flames and become one with fire. This is your moment to dance, so shapeshifter dance!

CHAPTER ELEVEN

Embracing Chaos as Magick

When I first began this chapter, I had already written eight chapters – a flow and the near-completion excitement kept me going. It was a Thursday morning in December when I typed up the chapter number and title. I remember taking a deep breath and asking myself: "How does one truly embrace chaos as magick?"

My computer immediately crashed. Thinking "oh it's just an old Apple Mac," I attempted to shut it down and restart to allow it to reboot. Only, it didn't reboot. After several attempts, and each time the loading screen would appear and just spin but never load, a panic began to surface. I had written almost 60 pages, my previous chapters were all almost near completion and just about ready for their final touch ups before sending off to the editor.

Anxiety is chaos within the body. Phone calls were made to friends who work with computers, my sister (who is liquid calm) was called and finally it was decided that my ancient computer needed to be taken into the computer repair shop with the hope that at least my files could be retrieved.

On Saturday, the prognosis was hopeful – my computer turned on and they were going to start moving the files onto a new hard drive. However, come Monday when I went to pick up my computer, no one knew the status – the afternoon workers seemed to not have any answers for me or a computer. So, Tuesday rolled around and when the computer tech said, "I have bad news," my heart sank to my stomach, my head dropped and my body crouched down to the floor. The hard drive had crashed during transfer and my files were forever lost and irretrievable.

How does one truly embrace chaos as magick? Well, it took me a few hours and days to see the irony of this being the particular chapter I was starting when my computer crashed. Was Loki playing a trick on me? Did Loki crash my computer? I cannot confirm nor deny. Either way, I was being presented with chaos and now the challenge of embracing this situation as magick began. Could I take this situation and apply it as lessons to help me embrace this chaos? Of course!

FIRST LESSON – DON'T REACT. JUST BREATHE.

When faced with chaos, it is often our initial reactions that trigger a domino effect that could result in either a negative or positive outcome. In this situation, the damage was done. I could beat myself up for not saving my files onto a flash drive or emailing them to myself (which I was going to do once I had completed the chapter I was working on) OR I could take the computer into the professionals and hope that they could salvage things. With the files not being able to transfer due a fried hard drive, my ultimate second reaction was: do I toss the book or start over?

My friend Amy didn't quit, even on the days where she was so sick from the chemo she passed out. I was not going to quit. I took a deep breath, let my initial reactions exhale out and there I was basically writing my entire book all over again. I was immediately transported back to chapter one and my own words thrust into my face: "If you invite a shattering and expect things to not break, that is completely on you. There is no one outside of self to blame."

SECOND LESSON – ADAPT!

Inviting chaos into my life is inviting things in my life to shatter and break. This is what chaos does. It breaks things into pieces so that we can either rebuild or let the pieces lie. After spending thirteen months with Loki energy shattering almost every aspect of my life, I was not going to stop now.

Bring it on chaos!! The song, *Unstoppable*, by Sia became my warrior song.

By definition of "adapt" means: to become adjusted to new conditions. My new condition being my previously intended book, which was now drifting in the chaos of the cosmos, never to be seen again. So here I am attempting through actions to make or alter this book into something more powerful, more suitable and more intuitively inspired. Thanks Loki, for crashing my computer so at least I can test my capabilities when it comes to adapting.

THIRD LESSON – DON'T DWELL.

We have all heard the quote by Bill Keane: "Yesterday is history, tomorrow is a mystery, today is a gift of God, which is why we call it the present." I sat with this quote and really tried through the ability of adapting to see this situation as a gift. I really sat with it, held it in my hands and heard: "Let it go." No, I cannot magically make my first draft of this book reappear in its original glory. No amount of tears will make the files come through a fried up hard drive. Embodying this third lesson will help me to move forward and not dwell on the "I should have or could have." Nope, not going to dwell.

If chaos is the ultimate teacher and pushes us as individuals to create order in our lives, why do we resist and fear it? Things happen on a daily basis that are not ideal or planned. They happen, which is why they have humorous bumper stickers and slogans such as "shit happens" – to remind us to not dwell but to adapt and keep the momentum going.

Trust me, I thought long and hard about not finishing this book. The thoughts: "People don't want a book about Loki, people hate chaos, no one was going to read it anyways" kept playing on repeat in my brain. But the truth is as an author that my writing is my therapy, it is my legacy for my future generations and yes there are people who are hungry for a book about Loki, people who embrace chaos as a magick – and someone will read it, even if it's only my mom.

When you invite chaos, there are moments that shake you. Writing a book about Loki is inviting chaos! The computer incident shook me to my core. Temporarily shattered me! However, for every incident, there is always a choice of how to react. So, I went home with the decision to apply the three lessons and begin the process of writing my book all over again. Even though I did not want to – a choice was made. No amount of looking back was going to propel me forward. I sat down at my laptop and began … again.

The next day, I received a call from the computer repair shop saying that I could come pick up my dead computer and the hard drive which, hopefully, some of my 20 years of files and pictures would be able to be saved from. I had every intention of taking my computer to the shooting range for some much-deserved target practice.

When I arrived, the computer tech said, "Hey, I have some really good news." Just yesterday, this same tech told me my computer was fried and my book files were irretrievable so his mention of good news baffled me. He went on to say that when he arrived at work this morning, my computer was on and opened to a page that said "book recovery" – he clicked on the button and my book files opened up. He then immediately transferred them over to the hard drive!

The only response I could give was to laugh! "Are you kidding me right now?!" The computer tech went on to say that he had never seen anything like this happen before. He said, "You are writing a book about Loki right, the God of Mischief?" My reply was yes. He laughed then and said, "Maybe we are all being played by the gods."

There was no explanation for the computer incident other than mischief and chaos at play. While this past thirteen months has triggered an agnostic response for me in many aspects, I have to agree with the computer tech when he said, "I've never been a big believer in gods but this incident with your computer shook me!"

Somewhat hesitant, I collected my computer and new hard drive and headed home. My hands were shaking and I felt an electric energy moving through me, making me a bit nauseous. When I plugged the hard drive into my computer, my book file was there! Not a single sentence was missing!

When I called my daughter to give her the crazy news, she just laughed and said, "Wow, Mom. It's like Loki was waiting to see if you would quit. Once you decided to just keep writing, he gave your book back." Even my Luv said, "It must have been a test – a test to see if you would quit or keep going, even if it meant starting over."

How many times in our lives are we given moments of chaos that ask us the same thing? Are you going to quit or keep going, even if it means starting over? Determination and perseverance are big super powers. I had accepted defeat and gave thanks for the lesson. I knew that I couldn't magically make the lost files reappear. I knew that I couldn't just give up and not write the book. I'd been riding chaos for thirteen months. My time, the energy invested and Loki was worthy of a book of devotion. Thank the powers that be, my files magically reappeared.

When my introduction states that I have embraced chaos as a lover, I mean that! No amount of scheduling, planning and control has taught me an ounce of what chaos has. Exerting power over every detail and attempting to dictate the outcome by controlling the fine details only left me feeling drained and disappointed.

Chaos is not a gentle lover – at least, not all the time. Chaos is the lover that abruptly seizes, thrusts you into a dark room, pulls your hair and gives you unexpected pleasure, sometimes in the aftermath. Chaos is both the good and the bad, always unpredictable and surprising. Chaos can be the gentle lover that surprises you with softness when you expect the opposite.

Looking back at these thirteen months, I see lovers' quarrels, pockets of assumed betrayal and rejections, but here in the moment I feel orgasmic delight. Fear and control did not taint my thirteen months of invited chaos, they only challenged me to either fight or take flight.

FOURTH LESSON – SURRENDER!

Once I had decided to just sit down and begin the process of writing my book once again from scratch, my files suddenly and quite honestly magically reappeared. Do I believe this was just a fluke? No! This incident with my computer softened my agnostic and atheist angst. It made a believer out of me. I felt like I was a pawn in the game of Loki.

By choosing to surrender, I stopped fighting the current and simply let circumstances carry me on the waters of possibilities. Whether those waters were calm or choppy, the outcome was going to be determined by my reactions.

We hear all the time: "Let go and let be." In fact, these were some of the last words I spoke to my friend as she was dying. She didn't need my permission or my words but by expressing them out loud they became an assurance that either way her body was done fighting and it was time to accept, time to surrender. Chaos cannot be controlled. It can only be resisted or embraced by the individual.

Embracing chaos as magick is defined in the Pagan practice as: "Ritualizing one's spiritual intentions." This use of the "k" at the end of the word was made popular by none other than Aleister Crowley, who wanted to differentiate his practices in the realm of alchemy and the Craft as something very distinctly abstract from stage magic.

Magick in chaos is seeing the magic in one's life through the eyes of a spiritual practitioner. We create rituals every day, why not embrace that rather than put on a facade or show? In Paganism, ritual techniques that change a person's consciousness so that they may better perceive and participate in divine reality are regarded as magick.

Changing one's consciousness begins with the individual choosing HOW they will perceive and participate. If we as individuals see chaos as a teacher, a friend, an opportunity or a Lover then we are shifting our conscious reactions to chaos and we will create a new outcome.

If Loki energy is that *internal/external jolt* as one goes from hot water to freezing, then we have to choose to either react with panic or breathe in with surrender.

If you have ever taken a cold plunge then you understand the physical and mental process of relaxing through the freezing cold temperatures that cause your brain to question your sanity. The first response, that *jolt*, is to gasp. However, once you choose to surrender to the cold then the healing powers of the freezing temperatures begin and you can actually relax, breathe calmly and trust that your body can adapt in this state of chaos.

A note of caution when embracing chaos: one's norm of chaos will shift. What was chaotic to me ten years ago has become everyday mundane. With age comes growth and the ability to see things that are occurring with a bit more patience (hopefully). Expecting the unexpected does help in diminishing the surprise and shock factor for sure. Just know that with this acceptance of chaos, your definition of chaos will shift as well.

CHAPTER TWELVE

The Unexpected Mother

Loki as Mother? When it comes to gender and assigned gender roles, the gods in myths and sagas are above such mere human things. Gender is a construct that we as humans have created. Loki is one god and individual that is not going to be bound to constructs, especially when it comes to gender.

Loki is a shapeshifter and as such he is able to transform his physical form into animals, insects and other human-type forms. Loki is also one to meddle and embrace his role as catalyst.

During a wager that had the Goddess Freya as a reward, Loki shifted into a mare in an effort to distract a Giant's stallion. His distraction was of a sexual manner and resulted in Loki giving birth to an eight-legged horse, Sleipnir. This act of birthing makes Loki a mother, not a father!!! In doing research, it baffles me that sources still gender-specify Loki as the father of this eight-legged horse despite the fact that Loki held this foal within a womb and birthed the foal in the traditional and natural manner. Loki is the MOTHER of Sleipnir.

LOKI GIVES BIRTH TO MORE THAN JUST A COUNTER-OFFER:

Odin wanted to protect his realm by constructing a wall around his territory – a wall so tall and strong that it would prevent even the frost giants from penetrating. Loki challenged this request by expressing that a wall of such magnitude and strength would take years to accomplish! Odin insisted.

Like most myths, a stranger just randomly appeared and with him was a large stallion called "Svadilfari". This stranger said that he could build such a wall in only three seasons. He promised to build such a wall the most skilled and fierce Gant could not breach. Odin, not being dumb, asked what this stranger wanted in return for building such a wall.

The stranger replied that he would only require three things in exchange for building this wall in three seasons – a winter, summer and one more winter. The first thing this stranger required was the hand of the Goddess Freya in marriage; the second thing he wanted was the Sun that rose in the sky each day; and the third being the Moon that rose each night.

Odin chuckled. The hand of Freya was no small thing and Freya might not agree to being used as a prize. Odin asked the stranger to step outside so he and the other gods, including a very angry Freya, could discuss things. The gods were all in outrage and all agreed that offering up Freya, the Sun and the Moon was too high a price – all but one. Loki had a counter-offer.

Loki's counter offer included some trickery and, of course, a bit of chaos. He proposed that they use this stranger to get the foundation of the wall built, but only in one season as opposed to three. Loki too did not believe in the stranger's ability but also wanted to appease Odin by helping to get this wall started. After this one season of uncompleted work, they could happily dispose of the stranger and not have to pay him any of three most precious requests.

The gods agreed to propose this to the stranger, with the stipulation that only this stranger and no one else could build this wall. This would ensure the stranger's failure, for how could one man build such a wall in just one season?

The stranger gave this some thought and countered with, "Can my horse help me with hauling the large stones?" Odin deemed this to be reasonable and so the deal was made. The very next day, the stranger began to work, with an audience of doubting gods watching on. The stranger dug deep trenches and in the evening he and his horse rode off with an empty sleigh to be filled with rocks.

Loki chuckled and did his best to comfort Freya by expressing that no one person and one horse could possibly fill that sleigh with heavy stones in less than a week. Freya remained angry and doubtful.

To the shock and surprise of everyone, the stranger and his stallion arrived with the dawn with a full sleigh full of heavy stones. This was impossible!

The stranger stacked stones by day and he and his stallion hauled stones at night. The wall was beginning to take form and each passing day of progress brought more and more fear to the gods. They did not want to lose Freya, the Sun or the Moon. Their anger began to take shape in the form of blame. Freya stated that if this wager was lost and she was to be a prize, her one request and consolation would be to see Loki killed for his arrogance and trickery. After all, Loki had suggested this new wager and quickly the gods forgot that they were accountable for their choice to agree – how convenient.

Loki, being faced with death, once again thought up a solution. On the eve of completion and the last day before the new season, Loki shifted into a mare. While the stranger was preparing to harness the stallion and go retrieve their last load of stones, the stallion caught sight and scent of the mare and ran off in a chase. No amount of yelling and whistling could get the stallion's attention. Both the stallion and mare disappeared in the forest.

In desperation and fierce frustration, the stranger tried to haul the sleigh himself – but he failed. He could only pull *a handful of stones, and a handful of stones was not going to complete the wall. As the Sun rose the next morning, he lost the wager. The stranger revealed that he was really a Mountain Giant and had his stallion not run off, he would have been able to complete the wager and would have been leaving with Freya, the Sun and the Moon.*

The Mountain Giant began to threaten Odin and the gods, screaming that they were nothing but oathbreakers and cheats. In his anger, he rushed at Odin only to be met with a flying hammer from none other than Thor, who had magically appeared at the very moment of need. The Mountain Giant was crushed by the might of Thor's hammer.

The gods themselves completed the last small section of the wall. Loki, however, did not return to bask in the glory of leading the stallion away. It was rumored that a lovely mare was seen out in the valley on the outskirts of the forest, but no sign of Loki.

About a year later, Loki did return and with him was an eight-legged foal. This foal followed Loki everywhere with great affection – the affection any child would bestow upon its mother – for Loki was just that: the mother. Loki named the foal Sleipnir.

Sleipnir grew to be the fastest and strongest horse. Faster than the wind! Loki gifted Odin Sleipnir.

Being cunning and creative is Loki's way of handling a situation. He knows no bounds and is willing to sacrifice his very body, reputation and put his life at risk in order to tempt the fates. This is one of my favorite Loki stories. He was quick to act and fix what could have been a very dire mistake, had he not intervened. This act of disregarding imposed gender roles gives Loki a new quality worthy of admiration. We humans have chosen to be bound by society's stipulations surrounding gender. As a woman growing up in Utah, it was heavily drummed into dogma (especially throughout the dominant religion) that a woman's place was in the home; barefoot and pregnant. While the man was to be the head of the household, sole provider and come home to be doted on by his endearing wife. Excuse me while I profusely vomit!

These roles that we have allowed to be shoved down our throats and deemed as acceptable are in fact extremely toxic and have contributed to the rise in suicide, anti-depressants and, quite naturally, divorce.

Women and men have unique and distinct physical differences, but to adopt the roles that society has placed upon male and female is a disservice to our ability to adapt. We mere humans are, after all, creatures beyond capable when it comes to adapting. We are seeing more and more men, by assigned gender, take on the role of sole parent in the home – shifting, happily, the construct that only women belong in the home.

Loki is the ultimate mirror, for his nature of challenging the norm is a catalyst that provides permission and a spark for us to do the same. We can challenge the norm. More and more individuals are choosing to ditch the labels, roles and imposing boxes that society has set for them and create intense inclusive shifts.

The role of mother includes more than just growing a fetus within a womb and birthing the baby. *Mother* is an archetype. In the modern world, we see the mother figure being celebrated by different earth-based practitioners, individuals and Christians. This mother figure is called many names, such as Gaia, Mary, Brahma, Leto, Cybele, Isis and Frigg, to name but a few.

What makes these figures mothers? Well, for starters – we do, as humans. Those who have written or carved myths and sagas have attached the title of mother to these and hundreds more deities, simply because humans wrote the myths and sagas.

Mother, as an archetype, possesses unique qualities that are defined by actions and characteristics. Mother by definition is directly attached to the physical birthing process, but there is more to it than that. A person can become pregnant and give birth, but not be a mother. Think of your own mother. What makes her stand apart? If you were to make a list of her unique characteristics and actions, would they isolate her as The Mother Goddess in your life? Or have you embraced those characteristics in someone else who has more fittingly embraced and taken on that role?

This is a question that can only be answered by the individual, as not everyone is going to have the same response, nor will they have the same relationship with the person who birthed them. My mother birthed six children, with me being the very last. She was not perfect by any means but whose mother really is? She did, however, provide for me, inspire me and help me to obtain the tools in life to be a successful individual. She was the first goddess-type figure in my life – followed by my grandmother.

When we apply the story of Loki as mother, we begin to break down those societal constricting roles and we can see in ourselves, the individual, how we can mother ourselves. If mother is connected to nurturing, protecting and caring-for as common attributes then can't we begin to nurture, protect and care for ourselves a bit more?

We tend to be told that Loki is simply a mischievous bastard whose only goal is to wreak havoc and cause mayhem. When we are shown him as mother, we are given an opportunity to see him in a nurturing light. We can once again see the human side that we as humans can relate to. When we humanize the gods, or those figures that we have been told are gods, we can establish and create a functioning relationship with not the actual deity but their attributes.

Loki was the unexpected mother. He could have easily shifted back into human-form after his night of trickery with the stallion. He could have chosen to NOT endure being pregnant as a horse, but he stuck with his decision and he followed through with the gestational period and birth of Sleipnir.

This is something that I greatly admire about Loki. He is comfortable in the uncomfortable. He embraces the unknown chaos of his own creations. He is fluid. He chose to become a mare and sexually distract the stallion. He accepted the consequence and, once again, he created another magical gift for Odin. That is quite a bit to be celebrated and something to honor.

It may be difficult to go from seeing Loki as trickster, chaos, catalyst and the ultimate mischief-making baddie to a nurturer, provider and compassionate mother. This is the magic of Loki. He is all, as we are all.

IN YOUR OWN LIFE:

- How are you embracing the lessons that you have created through chaos?
- How are you choosing to be both catalyst and mother?
- Can you see the power in nurturing your ability to adapt and break down the barriers that society has imposed?
- Are you willing to accept and honor, without blame, that you chose to play into those roles?
- Can you honor the gender-assigned women in your life as mother figures? Are you willing to love their strengths and see that you too possess the same, despite the physical distinctions?

CHAPTER THIRTEEN

Father of Monsters

Loki begins to be humanized tragically once his children come into play. Loki has six children, one of which we know is Sleipnir – the eight-legged horse who Loki is the mother to. He has two sons from his marriage with Sigyn; and three children not so fondly referred to as "monsters". The last three were birthed by the Giant and rumored witch, Angrboda: his daughter Hel, wolf-son Fenrir and the giant snake Jormungandr.

Odin, aware of the sons of Sigyn, is more preoccupied with the latter three – for Odin has a bad dream or a premonition about Loki's three children. This dream shakes him so badly that he sends Thor and Tyr to the Realm of Giants to brutally retrieve Loki's children.

When they reach Angrboda's dwelling, they are both in shock and revulsion when they see the three children or rather monstrous creatures. Hel, a small girl who appears alive and thriving on the right side of her body, is seen to be dead and decaying on the left side of her body. She is not afraid when taken by force to stand in front of the Allfather Odin. In fact, she is rather polite. When Odin asks her if she is either dead or alive, her response is: "I am but myself, daughter of Loki and Angrbodr." In discussion with Odin, Hel admits an affinity and great respect for the dead because they talk to her and treat her with more respect and kindness than the living.

Odin decides to make Hel the Ruler of the Dead – Queen of the Underworld and Dark Realm. Those who died outside of battle were to enter her realm, as the fallen warriors were instead sent to Valhalla. This seemed to please Hel, as she smiled at Odin and accepted her fate.

Jormungandr the serpent was met with fear. For this snake-child grew at a rapid pace and just in the time that he had been taken from his mother he had almost tripled in size. This was frightening to the Aesir and Odin. Odin tossed Jormungandr into the waters of the sea that surrounded Midgard. At least in the Water Realm, Jormungandr was not a threat. Jormungandr became the Great Serpent of Midgard; he grew so large he could encircle all of Midgard, head to tail.

Two of Loki's monstrous children were now dealt with. One sent to live in the deepest waters and the other to live in the deepest depths, welcoming the dead. Now the third child was the most incredible threat. Odin's dream had shown him that this particular child would bring about the end of all things.

Fenrir was a gray and black wolf pup when he was stolen. Each day, he grew at a rapid pace. At first he was small like a regular pup, but after a day he was about the size of a full grown wolf, then the next day the size of a bear, then the day after that he was the size of the largest elk. The Aesir were uncomfortable with the rapid growth rate of this wolf who could speak like a human – all but Tyr, who had taken a fondness for Fenrir ever since he first took him from his mother. Tyr was often seen to play with the wolf, pet him and talk to him often like a caring uncle.

Odin took his fear and dream of premonition to the other gods and a vote was cast. It was decided that Fenrir would be bound. It took some trickery. The gods taunted Fenrir by teasing him, telling him that he couldn't be bound and to break the chains. Fenrir, being incredibly strong, took the teasing to heart and said that he could in fact break any bond. So begin the bonding of Fenrir. Three times the gods bound him and three times Fenrir broke the chains. Fenrir thought that he was earning the approval of the gods but he was wrong. Odin went to the Dwarves to seek their assistance in crafting an unbreakable tether. The Dwarves agreed and created *"Gleipner"* – a ribbon incapable of breaking. By this time, Fenrir had grown suspicious.

Odin recognized Fenrir's apprehension and asked if Fenrir would trust his friend Tyr to bind him with Gleipner to test his strength? While Fenrir trusted Tyr, he still felt there was trickery. So Fenrir said he would agree to test the strength of Gleipner if a great warrior agreed to place his arm within Fenrir's mouth. This way, if Fenrir was betrayed and tricked, he could at least bite the arm off a great warrior, and surely Odin would not risk a great warrior to lose his arm?

Tyr volunteered to place his arm within Fenrir's mouth. The gods bound Fenrir with the Dwarves' woven cord Gleipner and Fenrir could not break the bond. He was bound. He was tricked. He was not only stolen from his mother and his siblings taken from him but now he was betrayed by the Aesir that had given him this new home and cared for him. Fenrir snapped Tyr's hand completely off.

Odin and the gods tethered Fenrir and dragged him fighting and snarling to a distant location, far from Asgard. Fenrir in his well-deserved wrath swore vengeance and promised to kill Odin for his betrayal and abuse. One of the gods struck Fenrir in the mouth with his sword, wedging Fenrir's mouth open as the sword stuck between his the lower and upper jaw, forcing Fenrir's mouth to remain uncomfortably open. The gods simply laughed at Fenrir and walked away, leaving him in a river of his own drool, in pain with the agony of betrayal and trickery.

In the book, *The Witches Heart*, written by Genevieve Gornichec, you are introduced to Angrboda (the witch who is the mother of Loki's children) in a positive light. This book tugged at all my heart strings. I cried through most of it, due to beautiful writing and the humanization of Loki. The reader really gets to see Loki as father, husband and man.

This book also highlights a side of Loki, who was present for the birth of these children: a father who loved them. When we look back at the myths and sagas, the common antagonist is Loki but is it really? The gods were terribly jealous and they never wanted to admit fault, so Loki was to blame for everything. The gods abused Loki, attempted to kill him numerous times and viciously attacked his children, tortured them and banished them.

As a mother, my heart aches. Ironically, I have three children; one daughter and two sons. My affinity is naturally for the outcast Giantess Angrboda, who watched her children being dragged by chains and tethers away from her to meet an unfortunate fate. As a father, can you imagine your children being tracked down and hunted, taken from their mother, banished – all because of a dream?

Odin may be the wise Allfather but his actions of abuse to Fenrir ultimately would lead to his dream being fulfilled. One should ponder what would have happened had the gods left Loki's children alone. Would Fenrir have had a desire for revenge against Odin in the first place? No!

Loki is father to six children according to myths and sagas. In his marriage to Sigyn, he has two sons, *Narfi* and *Vali*. These two sons ultimately were punished by the gods because of their father's treacherous attack on Baldr. The contradiction and hypocrisy amongst the gods is ever prevalent.

Loki's children could be stolen, tethered and abused without thought of consequence, but the same treatment was not even to be thought of in consideration. Hmmmm. Makes one wonder who the real antagonists are?

When we move through the myths and sagas, we see Loki in almost every stage from young and mischievous to adult, to father and even mother. These stories make his progression and our own relatable. This is the power of looking to deities such as Loki as teachers, messengers and gods. Who wants to pray to a god who has never experienced upheaval and the chaos of a mortal existence?

Growing up with the Mormon religion, there was this concept of a God or Heavenly Father who never lived an actual life, who never struggled or felt chaos but was perfect? How? I suppose floating on a cloud, only observing but yet demanding perfection from those on Earth made him a father figure? There are so many things wrong and contradictory about the Christian God. Give me Loki: an openly fucked up figure who has actually experienced the ups and downs. Him I can relate to.

Whether you have children or not, it is safe to say that everyone can empathize with what one would do in Loki's situation(s). As a mother, he gave up his son Sleipnir as a gift to Odin. As a father, he watched his two sons with Sigyn tortured, he then watched his three children with Angrboda deemed monsters and tortured as well. What would you do? How would you feel? How would you react?

As a mother, first-hand: if someone comes after my children there will be a reckoning! Mothers are notorious and frightful in their instinctual protection of their children. Fathers too! Don't mess with kids. That's law!

For some though, Loki is still the bad guy! Despite seeing him as the bringer of light, the nurturing mother, friend and the only constant companion. There are some who believe the myths and sagas so much that they continue to demand justice for the gods and attack Loki and anyone who looks at him in a positive light – as if Loki somehow deserves all that the gods inflict upon him. Attacking his children though, that's low! No matter what I do, my children are not to be held accountable for my actions. In movies and books, we always want the little guy to win, right? We root for the underdog. Loki is the underdog! Quite literally the coyote in the wolf pack.

The gods are a pack and Loki is the unworthy and unwanted. It is interesting to me how many modern-day Heathens and Pagans forget that they are the underdogs too. It is easy to jump on a bandwagon, ditch one's personal ideas and morals to be welcomed by the pack of popularity.

I consider myself fortunate as I have always been an underdog, unwanted by many, rejected for my wildness and dismissed for my individuality. However, for me, my authenticity has always been my superpower. The pack of popularity never really appealed to me. They were a force in numbers but as individuals outside their pack they were weak.

Loki stands the test of time. He is constantly rejected by the pack and yet he still manages to reign supreme. So powerful in his own making that the gods have to lower themselves and attack children. That, right there, speaks volume as to their character.

In *The Witches Heart*, the reader really gets to see the pain and agony that Loki endures at the humor of the gods. He is a man, a lover, father and someone who aches to be recognized as Odin's brother. I cannot express enough how loved and cherished this novel is.

Loki is the underdog that you want to win, but we all know the outcome. We all know the suffering that is thrust upon Loki – his undoing.

Am I alone in wanting Loki to be the good guy, to avenge his children? I don't think so.

Lokeans and those who root for the underdog will want Loki to fight back. We need him to fight back. In some way, it justifies our own actions when it comes to how we defend and fight for our own children. Loki MUST stand up to the gods and protect his children, even the monsters.

THE DEATH OF BALDER – POSSIBLY A FATHER'S REVENGE

Balder the bright and shining one, most beloved and cherished son of Frigga & Odin. Balder who never did anything wrong. The literal golden child had bad dreams, omens that foretold the end. He would wake up afraid and worried. Many overheard these dreams, most worried. Not Loki.

Frigga and Odin went to great lengths and traveled far to ensure the safety of their precious Balder. Frigga went to every creature and person, demanding a sworn oath that nothing would harm her son. Odin sought council in his wanderings. He met with Hel, Loki's daughter, who informed him that death was coming to her kingdom and with it, Balder.

In their desperation, Odin and Frigga both came upon an old woman who offered counsel and overheard much. She told Odin that Balder would reach his end. She heard Frigga express that all plants were promised to not hurt Balder – all but mistletoe, which wasn't worth anyone's time or oath.

This old woman was Angrboda, were she and Loki seeking revenge for their children? Maybe? Loki, being wise and cunning, watched all this take place. He watched as the other gods and warriors tested Frigga's oaths. They beat up Balder, threw stones at him, hit him with trees and an assortment of plants. Nothing could hurt him. They seemed to make a sport of it and put on a good show.

Hod, the blind brother of Balder, was irritated and couldn't participate. Loki seized the opportunity and gave Balder an arrow, the head of which had been dipped in mistletoe. Loki encouraged Hod to shoot the arrow and participate in the sport of testing Balder's invincibility – Loki even offered to help him aim.

The arrow was shot; Balder was hit and instantly died. Hod, being blind, was not to be held accountable. Frigga wailed in the agony the way that only a mother could. Odin was distraught and all the gods wept. Balder would make the journey to Hel and take a seat at her table in her hall in the Underworld.

There are many different yet similar versions of this tale. "Brothers pinned against brothers" is not a new theme. The bright and shining one, Balder, has been compared to Jesus – which would make the Loki as Lucifer concept even more ideal. Some believe that the gods knew that Loki was at fault or at least they suspected him of being involved. In some retellings, this is the end of Loki and his son's, Narfi and Vali.

LOKI'S PUNISHMENT

All the gods and people wept in despair following Balder's death. The Sun no longer seemed to shine and there was much crying and sorrow. Loki had no patience for this and was quite irritated by all the sobbing.

While feasting in the great hall, amongst the wailers, Loki took to drinking – a lot! So much that he started to really express his truths and he began to toss out insults. He became a mean and angry drunk. He took malicious jabs at the goddesses and the gods, and pretty much everyone in that great hall was attacked verbally by Loki's bitter tongue.

He left to sleep off his drunkenness. The gods had all had enough of Loki. His night of tossing out verbal attacks was just too much, so they set out to seize him. They took Loki into a deep cavern. Loki reminded them that they couldn't kill him. He was the oath-brother of Odin and was therefore untouchable.

Those who bound him laughed and said they were not going to kill him. They were, however, going to kill his sons. It was then that Loki saw Sigyn and his two sons Narfi and Vali bound. Loki's heart sank. Narfi and Vali were killed in front of Loki and Sigyn, their entrails made into tethers that were used on Loki as he was bound, arms outstretched between two stones.

Skadi entered the cave with a venomous snake that was placed at head height on the stones Loki was bound to. Each time he would move his head, the snake would spit burning poison onto his face. Sigyn, in her despair and out of love for Loki, retrieved a bowl and each time the snake would spit, she would catch the venom in the bowl to save Loki from the sting.

This by far is one of the cruelest and cringiest punishments. Every time I read the story or even think about it, it brings tears to my eyes. Can you imagine watching your children brutally tortured and killed in front of you and your spouse?

The heart-wrenching pain and agony – and both mother and father had to witness this brutality. Then to be bound by the entrails of your children! What horror!

As a mother, I cannot even begin to want to empathize with this evil attack, but it is important to ask oneself: does this punishment fit the crime? In my personal opinion, no! Loki as the black sheep, the outcast and underdog threw out a bunch of verbal attacks. Yes, he tricked Hod into shooting the mistletoe-dipped arrow but where does one consider Hod and his ability to think for himself? Hod could have chosen to not participate.

Loki was not perfect, not even remotely. He badgered, taunted and challenged the gods repeatedly but to take his children and those *monsters*, as they called them, and banish them was a bit harsh. Then to kill his sons in front of their mother and demand that Loki watch is a punishment unimaginable and so cruel. It bears the question: who were the real devils? Who were the real baddies? Who were the real monsters?

What we learn from Loki, as a father, is that he is flawed. Do you know of any father figure that isn't? But his children should not be held responsible for his shortcomings. Who are we as mere humans and who are the gods of the Aesir to act as judge and jury? Where does accountability come into play?

In the myths and sagas of (not only) Norse mythology, we see repeated themes: betrayal, jealousy, lust and retribution. Over and over again, we read repetitive stories of things gone wrong by ego-driven catalysts. Yet for most mere humans, we miss the metaphors and lessons. Maybe that's why we need so many repetitive stories? We begin to justify our behaviors and act just as irresponsible and reckless. We begin to think that we are the judge and jury.

We unfortunately recreate the myths in our own stories of life. We miss out on the opportunity to see that oftentimes the myths are warning us of what not to do, rather than what to do. Loki was punished in the myths and the stories – myths we know to be fictional. It is not our place to hold fictional characters accountable, as they didn't do anything to us. Loki didn't sit at my table and boast about what fuck-ups my family were. He didn't cut off my hair. He didn't break an oath with me.

As humans, we are capable of so much more! We can look at the myths and actually learn from them by seeing the perspective of not just the heroes but the villains as well because, quite frankly, we are at times villains too.

RAGNAROK – THE END OF ALL OR THE BEGINNING:

It has been prophesied that after the gods have long left this realm to slumber in a deep sleep and man has ruled for more decades then can be counted, a great winter will begin. This will be the winter of all winters. The Sun and Moon will be swallowed up and darkness will envelope the land. There will be no day; there will be no night – only darkness in a never-ending winter.

In this chill, battles will ensue. Brothers against brothers, fathers against sons, mothers against daughters, sisters against sisters. Lust, greed and ego will reign as the humans begin to self-destruct. This madness, this chaos will cause the earth to rumble and shake. The old gods will awaken from their deep sleep and put on their armor, pick up their swords and prepare for a war unlike any other.

Loki's tethers will crack and break, releasing him from the prison cave. His children Hel, Fenrir and Jormungandr will wage a counter-attack against the gods who banished them. Hel will raise an army of the dead and with Loki steering the massive ship they will sail from the underworld on the rocky waves of the vast sea.

Jormungandr will cause the waters to tremble and erupt along the shores, wiping out most of the land as he encroaches towards the shore. Fenrir will run at full speed and charge against Odin Allfather, his hackles raised and his teeth bared. The great World Tree will shake as the mighty wolf runs. Odin, with his spear in hand, will charge at the wolf, riding none other than Fenrir's half-brother, Sleipnir. As Odin encroaches upon Fenrir, the mighty wolf opens his jaw and swallows the Allfather whole. Vidar, son of Odin, who witnessed the death of his father, will attack Fenrir with a vengeance so powerful that the wolf is killed as Vidar rips the wolves jaw in two.

Thor rides towards the sea serpent and smashes the giant snake with his mighty hammer, Mjolnir. As the blow crushes the snake's head, venom spews like an erupting volcano and covers Thor, killing him instantly. Both snake and Thor lie dead, side by side.

Loki will turn his attack on Heimdall who foretold all, who saw all. Loki will gloat and shout that he has triumphed! He will celebrate the death of the gods.

Heimdall and Loki will offer each other a lethal blow. Side by side, they lie in their blood – battle, destruction, death and chaos surrounding them. As Loki dies, Heimdall offers him no solace, only the reminder that with all death there is new life. What seems like an ending is really a beginning. The gods achieved nothing beyond lives spent preventing the end

*that they feared yet would come, no matter what they did.
Loki's reign of chaos would end and with it the chaos of new
beginnings would erupt.*

Were Loki's children to be feared from the very beginning,
based on a prophecy of Ragnarok? Was Loki mistreated
time and time again because of his part in Ragnarok? A
Ragnarok that would possibly happen? Were they pawns in
a much larger game? It would seem so.

We all face the same ending in this existence. Death.
Whether we want to admit it, face it or acknowledge it.
Death will come for us all. It is our one and only guarantee.
Tragic and heartbreaking. All that will be left of us are the
stories that will be told – our stories, our triumphs, our
follies, our battles, our loves. We will all become legends
in the lives of those who walked beside us, battled with us
and loved us. Our end will become a new beginning. The
wheel of life will continue to turn. Our loved ones will have
to learn to keep going, despite our absence.

The holes we leave behind will become our legacies.
Some will leave holes so deep that they can never hope to be
refilled. We as humans will continue onward, searching for
ways to avoid the pain of the unavoidable. When my friend
left this realm and journeyed into her own underworld,
joining the realm of the dead, she left a void so large it often
feels like grieving her is a black hole with no escape – a
grief that sucks you in and holds you hostage in the dark
and never-ending winter. Grief is a new kind of chaos.

Loki, as a father, loved his children. He fought for them.
He died avenging them. Odin, as a father, did the same.
Thor, as a father, also did the same. We see strong masculine

figures that were each afraid of their death as prophesied in Ragnarok. They wanted to ensure a good death, one of their choosing and, ultimately, they failed in this quest.

Now it's up to us, the readers of the myths, legends, sagas and the stories. What do we do with these tidbits? We pick them apart; we cling to what gives us hope. We find bad guys and point fingers. We defend heroes who acted the same as villains. We critique, we construct and we formulate new meanings that give our lives purpose. We find things to relate to. Metaphors to mirror. Gods to worship. Devils to fear. The cycle repeats. We read the stories to our children, we warn them of apples and about eating forbidden fruits, we caution against falling prey to temptations. We teach our children how to recognize the baddies, who to fear, who to pray to. The cycle repeats.

Can we sit and see how the myths as metaphors have shaped us? Do we embrace chaos as a lover? Are we still looking for a catalyst to blame, a snake hidden in the grass? Is Loki still a bad guy? A trickster? Master of Mischief? Or is he a father? A husband? A mirrored reflection of our imperfect selves? A giant who longed for acceptance from his peers, not for who he could be but for who he already was?

As a parent, a grandparent and one who is living chaos and experienced deep loss and profound love, I can honestly say that I hope there is a lesson to be found in the madness – an acceptance of the good and bad, for they both reside within. It is my hope that we as individuals can write our own uniquely flawed and glorious stories as only we know how so that our future generations will feel as if they can know us as legends, as giants and as gods!

In the past thirteen chapters, you have met Loki as catalyst, chaos, wildfire, coyote, oathbreaker, father, mother and opener of doors. Are you ready to shake things up, dance around the unpredictable flames, be brave, be bold, embrace your own inner wildness and dare to be mischievous? Can you swim against the stream of comfort and light a spark?

Be the catalyst in your own life. Create your own definition of chaos! Live your own story as only you know how.

Happy Writing.

– Love, Lady Wolf

Helpful Resources:

- https://www.smithsonianmag.com/smithsonian-institution/folklorist-explains-lokis-place
- https://en.wikipedia.org/wiki/Lokasenna
- https://norse-mythology.org/tales/loki-and-the-dwarves/
- https://thenorsegods.com/loki/
- Youtube - coyote myth
- *What is Chaos Magic?* by Catherine Beyer
- *Animals as Gods* by Lady Wolf
- *Tarot for One* by Courtney Weber Hoover
- *Norse Mythology* by Neil Gaiman
- *Tales of Norse Mythology* by A.E. Keary
- *The Prose Edda* by Snorri Sturluson
- *Essential Asatru* by Diana L. Paxson
- *Viking Oracle Deck* by Stacey Demarco
- *Rune Oracle Deck* by Lo Scarabeo

Image: 2023 North Berwick Scotland – The Law

Lady Wolf resides in Southern Utah where, together with her Lover of 23 years, she offers animism anchored services to her community from the Desert Healing Sanctuary.

She is the mother of three and "Gigi" to two beautiful wild granddaughters. Lady Wolf began her journey into witchcraft at the age of sixteen. She is an initiated witch and triple ordained Wiccan priestess.

In 2017, she birthed her own witchcraft tradition: "Desert Sage Witchcraft" – a tradition devoted to the plants and animals of the High Desert of Utah. She is a reiki master, crystal therapist, green witch, hypnotherapist, chakra healer, initiated Bard, yoga instructor, Seidr, animist priestess and she also manages the local independent bookshop.

As a constant student, Lady Wolf splits her time between reading, running the bookshop, writing and honoring all the plants, animals and humans as teachers in her life. She graciously shares space with three dogs, three tortoises and five cats.

As an animist and shapeshifting priestess, Lady Wolf's passion is in helping individuals, couples and groups connect with animals as teachers, messengers and gods.

Since 2018, Lady Wolf has spent ample time retracing her ancestral roots in Scotland. She has spent several weeks in Edinburgh doing research for future books, embracing Paganism with the locals and also as a way of getting to know her family through the landscape they were born into.

To connect with Lady Wolf more:
- www.utahgoddesstemple.org
- desertsagewitchcraft@gmail.com
- youtube channel: @ladywolfauthor
- facebook: @ladywolfauthor OR @deserthealingsanctuary
- tiktock: ladywolf505readsalot
- instagram: @ladywolfauthor